Senior Kisses

# Kisses

# Senior Kisses

## by Diane Namm

**WESTWIND**

**Troll Associates**

Dedicated to Joanne Mattern, my editor,
who has made all the difference.

# Chapter One

*H*ero Montoya was the picture of impatience in his black leather motorcycle jacket, T-shirt, and jeans, as he leaned his broad, muscular back against Amanda Townsend's locker. He brushed back the one lock of his brown hair that always fell across his forehead, looking in vain for a glimpse of Amanda.

These days, it seemed as though he was forever waiting around for Amanda to finish up with yet another meeting of the dozens of committees to which she belonged.

Last year when they were sopho-mores, Hero was new in town, an out-sider. He had noticed the rich and beautiful Amanda Townsend mainly because she was always the center of some crowd's attention, always laughing unselfconsciously, and tossing her long ash-blonde hair over her shoulder. He'd even fallen in love with her, knowing that she could never be his. So Hero couldn't believe his good luck when they'd ended up working together at KSS-TV for the summer.

Nothing had prepared him for the fact that Amanda Townsend would fall in love with him, too.

The past few months had been the best and worst summer he'd ever had. Hero remembered their rides along the beach, the drive-in movies, Amanda's body melding with his when they rode on his motorcycle. A gentle smile played around Hero's lips as he thought about Amanda's soft mouth on his, and the way her long, silky hair brushed against his cheek when they kissed.

But a shadow fell across Hero's face when he thought of how Amanda's former best friend, Samantha Walker, had tried to break them up by flirting with Hero and lying to Amanda about Hero's interest in her. It had taken Hero a long time to get past the fact that Amanda had actually believed Samantha instead of him.

Just then, Hero caught sight of Amanda talking with Tyler Scott as they met on the path outside the lockers. As usual, Tyler looked like a perfect preppie in his senior varsity sweater, not a hair out of place. Hero's anger started to boil as he watched Amanda laugh at something Tyler said. Despite everything Tyler had done to Hero, Amanda insisted on maintaining their friendship.

"Tyler's changed. He's really sorry," Amanda had told Hero, along with a lot of other bull that Tyler had fed her.

The bottom line was that the Scotts and the Townsends were old family friends, and Amanda wasn't about to cut Tyler loose—certainly not for Hero.

Hero kicked his leather-clad toe into the crack between the wall and the lockers, staring at the yellow and orange leaves brushing against the window.

Amanda might be able to forgive Tyler, but Hero couldn't forget how Tyler had tried to drive him off a cliff during their motorcycle race at the Fourth of July Beach Bash. Or how Tyler had sabotaged the funding for KSS-TV and monkeyed with Hero's computer program at the KSS-TV station to make everyone think that Hero had stolen money from the KSS-Off Concert fund-raiser.

Hero was so intent on toeing the crack in the wall with the tip of his leather boot that he didn't notice someone standing right next to him, waiting for him to notice her.

"Hey, Hero, if you keep doing that, you're liable to bring the whole school down," a soft voice purred pleasantly into Hero's ear.

Hero looked up with surprise, then blushed when he realized that Melissa "Missy" Hanover, senior Homecoming Queen, had been standing there watching him for several minutes.

Missy was hard not to notice. Her soft, wavy auburn hair framed her pretty face. Her large green eyes stared with frank interest at Hero, and a smile hovered on her lips. Even Hero, who usually had eyes only for Amanda, wasn't totally oblivious to Missy's charms. He glanced approvingly over Missy's soft, curving shape, covered in a soft peach clingy sweater and short black skirt.

"Yeah, and if I brought the whole school down, where would that leave us?" Hero said with a teasing grin.

"Standing alone, together, amidst the rubble," Missy replied softly, moving closer to Hero. He didn't feel like moving back.

"So, what are you up to?" Hero asked.

"Oh, I was supposed to meet Tyler Scott at the library so we could study together . . ." Missy began.

At the mention of Tyler's name, Hero grimaced. "Better hurry, then. You wouldn't want to leave Tyler Scott waiting around," he replied, bitterness in his voice.

"Oh, Tyler's busy talking to Amanda Townsend. And time always stops for Tyler when he's talking to Amanda. Besides, I'm busy talking to you right now," Missy said casually, giving Hero a slow, seductive smile.

"So, what are you hanging around the lockers for?" Missy asked. "I would have thought you'd be out on the road, wind in your hair, racing that sexy motorcycle of yours along the beach."

"I'm just waiting for that very same Amanda."

"Oh, right. I forgot that you and Amanda had a thing. Pretty brave of Mandy to leave you all by yourself like this," Missy teased.

"Yeah, tell that to her," Hero joked back, flattered by Missy's attentions.

"Maybe I will," Missy answered. Then she looked at her watch. "Well, maybe Tyler's done flirting with Amanda by now," she said with a mischievous smile. "Any time you get tired of waiting around for Mandy Townsend, queen of the junior committee circuit, you just let me know." Missy touched Hero's arm lightly. "I'll meet you anywhere, anytime," she added.

Just before she walked away, Amanda came rushing down the hallway, her long ash-blonde hair tumbling around her sparkling violet eyes. She paused when she saw Missy Hanover and her Hero standing together, talking like they were old friends.

I didn't know Hero even knew Missy, Amanda thought to herself. Missy wasn't one of Amanda's favorite people. In fact, she and Missy had never liked each other, not even in grade school.

For a moment, seeing Hero standing so close to Missy, Amanda felt a pang of jealousy. Then she remembered what had happened this past summer, when Samantha had tried to make Amanda jealous over Hero, and she pushed her uneasy thoughts away.

Hero loved her, Amanda reminded herself. Holding her close, his strong hands caressing her back, Hero had told her over and over how no one and nothing would ever come between them.

But, when she saw Missy smiling at Hero—and Hero smiling back— Amanda couldn't help but wonder if that was still true.

"Hey, you," Amanda said, coming up behind Hero and putting her arms around his waist.

"Hey," Hero said, glancing back at Amanda. "Girl, where've you been?" Hero brought Amanda around so he could kiss her.

Amanda returned Hero's kiss, chills running through her body as his mouth hungrily sought and covered hers.

Catching her breath, Amanda stepped back a moment. Sometimes Hero's kisses were so intense, they made Amanda forget where she was.

"Where are you going?" Hero asked softly, bringing Amanda back in close.

"Come on, Hero, we don't have time. We have to get over to KSS or we'll be late for Drew's meeting," Amanda said, trying to ignore the slow hum in her body that Hero's kiss had awakened.

"And whose fault is it that we don't have any time together?" Hero asked, arching his eyebrow. "I've been waiting for you for over half an hour, just like I do every day. You spend

14

more time at committee meetings and yakking with your so-called friends, like Tyler Scott, than you do with me."

"Oh, please, spare me the guilt," Amanda said, withdrawing from Hero's arms. "We've been through all this before. Tyler did his penance, and the kind of stuff he pulled over the summer won't ever happen again. He promised. Besides, you didn't look like you were pining away from loneliness yourself," Amanda added pointedly.

"What does that mean?" Hero asked, his eyes narrowing.

"You know what it means," Amanda replied. "Missy Hanover was hanging all over you. Did you think I wouldn't notice?"

Hero scowled. "I don't know what you're talking about. But I don't imagine you notice much about me, since you're never around when you say you will be, anyway," Hero remarked coldly.

"Oh, Hero, let's not fight," Amanda said. "I'm sorry I said that about Missy, and I'm sorry I was late. Tyler's working with me on the planning committee so he was walking me over here, and they just elected me chairman, and now I have all this stuff to do for the homecoming and . . . "

"Hey, forget it," Hero said, putting his arm around Amanda's shoulder. "Come on, let's get going before we're late for the KSS meeting too." Hero guided her toward the door and out to the parking lot where his motorcycle was parked.

Expertly, Amanda fastened her monogrammed white helmet—Hero's one-month anniversary gift to her. She swung onto the motorcycle, fitting her body against Hero's as he gunned the engine.

"Do you think Missy Hanover is pretty?" Amanda asked as they were about to take off.

"What?" Hero asked, not able to hear over the roar of the engine.

"Never mind," Amanda shouted back.

Don't be ridiculous, she thought to herself. Don't do this to yourself all over again.

As Hero pulled the motorcycle away

from the curb, he caught sight of Missy Hanover waving to him through the library window. Hero responded with a short nod and a slight wave, then turned the cycle around to exit the school lot.

Catching the brief exchange, Amanda felt troubled. Could Hero actually fall for trouble like Missy Hanover?

After catching the glimpse of Missy at the library window, Hero was wondering exactly the same thing.

# Chapter Two

Keera Johnson was daydreaming as she headed for the KSS-TV station, where she worked along with Amanda Townsend, Hero Montoya, and Jamar Williams.

Keera closed her eyes and smiled as the image of Jamar floated before her eyes. She and Jamar had been going out now for over three months. And no one was more surprised about how long her relationship with Jamar had lasted than Keera was.

Jamar was so different from anyone Keera had known, she would never in a million years have picked him for a boyfriend. Between his friends and his band, JellyJam, Jamar barely had time to crack a book. Before she'd met Jamar, studying had been Keera's life.

For a while, during the summer,

their differences had almost meant the end of their love. Jamar's busy schedule had sent Keera back to her books, and she tried as hard as she could to freeze her heart against Jamar. And when Rogue, Jamar's best friend and lead singer in his band, tried get between Jamar and Keera, it seemed as though they were truly doomed.

But Keera's heart had melted after Jamar had written the awesome "Keera's Song" just for her and played it at the KSS-Off Concert.

Jamar was still always busy, since the JellyJam band had really taken off after playing with Nick Ganos and Grim Reaper at the KSS-Off Concert. Grim Reaper was planning to record "Keera's Song" for their next CD. And although Keera told herself that she really didn't mind, sometimes she wondered, if it weren't for their jobs at KSS-TV, how much she would ever get to see Jamar.

Lost in thought, Keera didn't hear the car horn tooting beside her as she walked.

"Hey, there," a voice called from the street.

Looking up, Keera saw a red convertible pull up beside her. Smiling and waving from inside was none other than Jordan Harris—a senior, and the star basketball player at Cliffside High.

Keera looked around, figuring Jordan must be speaking to someone else. But there was no one else around.

"Are you talking to me?" Keera managed to squeak.

"Of course I'm talking to you, girl. You're Keera, right?" Jordan asked.

Keera nodded shyly, surprised that Jordan Harris even knew she was alive, much less knew her name.

"Where are you off to in such a hurry, Keera?" Jordan asked.

"I'm on my way to work at the KSS-TV station over on Hillcrest," Keera said.

"Want a lift?" Jordan asked, leaning over to open the passenger side door.

"Sure, that would be great," Keera replied, her heart beating faster. She hoped that her excitement and surprise weren't showing.

"Cool," Jordan said as Keera stepped

into the car. As they drove along, Jordan gave Keera a long, appreciative look. He took in the soft black hair that curled around her face and her wide sea-green eyes.

"You know, Keera, you're even prettier up close than you are on TV," Jordan remarked.

Keera's face turned red.

"Did I embarrass you? I'm sorry, I didn't mean to," Jordan said.

"No, it's okay, thanks," Keera said faintly, recovering her composure.

"So how does it feel to be a tube celebrity?" Jordan teased.

Again Keera blushed.

"I mean it, I think your show is cool. How do you have time to work and stay on top of school, too?" Jordan asked. "I mean, what with practices and basketball games, I barely have a chance to check out my assignments."

"Well, it is hard," Keera started to say, seriously considering the question. "But, now that the SATs are over, I feel like I've got loads more time than I used to."

"Yeah—those SATs were a killer. I

have to retake chemistry this year, because I couldn't pass, what with SATs and then basketball. The coach and the principal let me slide last semester, but if I can't break a C, I'm really in for it this year," Jordan told her. "They'll kick me off the team for sure."

"Oh, no. That would be a disaster," Keera said sympathetically.

"Don't I know it," Jordan agreed, pulling up in front of the TV station.

Reaching for the door, Keera said in a low voice, "Thanks for the ride, Jordan."

"Wait one second, Keera," Jordan said, staying her with his hand. Then he jumped out and hurried over to open the car door, holding out his hand to help Keera out.

Flattered by Jordan's attentiveness, Keera placed her small, soft hand in Jordan's large, calloused palm.

Jordan smiled down into Keera's eyes as he closed his hand around hers.

"Well, thanks again, Jordan," Keera said, sliding past him to stand on the sidewalk.

"No problem," Jordan replied. "Maybe I'll see you around again soon."

Keera wondered if she was supposed to mention that she was seeing Jamar. Would Jordan think she was being a total dork, assuming that he wanted to go out with her when he was just being polite?

Before Keera could decide what to say, Jamar raced up on his bicycle, head bent, baseball cap pulled up high above his forehead, wearing neon-green bike shorts and a long T-shirt that flapped in the wind as he rode. His head was bopping up and down to the sounds on his Walkman. With a screech of his bicycle tires, Jamar pulled up right behind Jordan's car and jumped off.

"Hey, there, Keera, girl. Hey, guy." Then Jamar took a closer look. "You're Jordan Harris. How are you, man? Great season last year. You gonna do it again this year?" Jamar asked in a friendly way.

"I'm sure gonna try, if they let me," Jordan said, glancing back at Keera, who nodded sympathetically.

"Well, I have to be going," Jordan

said abruptly. "Maybe I'll hit the books for a while before practice." Jordan slid back into his car and drove off, waving to Keera.

"Hey, I didn't know you knew Jordan Harris," Jamar commented as he put his arm around Keera's shoulders and began walking toward the station door.

"I don't. I mean, I didn't, but now I do. I mean, he offered me a ride from school, that's all," Keera said, stumbling over the words.

"Don't be falling for any broad-shouldered basketball star and leaving me flat, okay?" Jamar joked, not really believing that Keera would.

"Don't be ridiculous, I hardly even know him." Keera smacked Jamar on the arm.

"Just kidding," Jamar told her, hugging her close. "Hey, guess what's going on next Friday night, the night before the Halloween dance?" Jamar asked excitedly.

Hoping against hope, Keera replied, "You've got no gigs, and we're going out, just the two of us?"

Jamar looked at Keera as though she had two heads.

"Are you crazy, girl? Why would I be excited about having no gigs? No, we're playing the Torch Club. Nick Ganos says it's the biggest scene in this part of the state. Nick got us the gig himself. Says it's where he got his big break a few years ago. You'll be there, right?" Jamar asked, not really doubting Keera's reply.

Thinking of how tired she was of sitting in the audience, one of a crowd, watching Jamar play, and then watching him party with his friends way into the night, Keera hesitated.

"You'll have to drive over yourself," Jamar continued, oblivious to Keera's hesitation. "But we'll be able to spend some time together between sets . . . and afterward," Jamar finished, his eyes gleaming with triumph.

This was the big break he'd been waiting for, and Keera didn't have the heart to spoil it for him. But she really couldn't stand the thought of another night out with the band. For no reason at all, Jordan Harris's face popped into

Keera's head. And the words, "Maybe I'll see you around again soon," burned in her brain.

"I'll see if I can make it," Keera told Jamar, opening up the station door and stepping inside.

"You'll see?" Jamar said, frowning with concern, as he followed Keera into the station.

"That's right," Keera said firmly, not looking at Jamar. "I'll see."

Jamar knew better than to press Keera further. But he wondered whether Keera's sudden hesitation had anything to do with Jordan Harris.

Keera was thinking the very same thing.

# Chapter Three

"*H*ey, Keera, Jamar. Where have you been? We've been waiting for you," Drew Pearson, the station manager, said, as he waved Keera and Jamar into his office. Amanda and Hero were already sitting on opposite ends of Drew's worn leather couch.

"What's up?" Jamar asked, plopping himself down in the middle of the couch. Keera seated herself on a chair across from Drew's desk and looked expectantly at Drew.

"What's up is, our financial sponsors, Scott Enterprises, called this morning and strongly suggested that we do a Halloween show for the end of this month's programming," Drew told them.

"Oh, groan," Keera said. "Who wants to watch Halloween stuff anymore?"

Hero and Jamar nodded in agreement. "Halloween is for kids."

"Well, we're stuck between a rock and a hard place, because our sponsors told me that, if we do a Halloween show, they'll double our funding for the year."

"Why would anyone at Scott Enterprises care whether or not we do a Halloween show?" Hero asked, wrinkling his forehead.

"Don't ask me—I'm just telling you what they said," Drew remarked. "And they told me to make it scary," he added.

"You know, the committee is doing a Haunted Homecoming theme for this year's homecoming party," Amanda said. "Maybe there's a way to tie the two things together."

"What do you mean?" Jamar asked with interest. After Amanda came up with the idea for last summer's KSS-Off Concert, Jamar was always up for any plan of Amanda's.

"Well, we're doing an old-fashioned kind of Halloween," Amanda said, her eyes sparkling and her cheeks flushing with color as enthusiasm rose in her voice. "We're going to have bobbing for apples, fortune-telling, prank booths, a horror funhouse, and anything else we can think of between now and then."

"Maybe we could do something on the history of Halloween?" Keera suggested.

Jamar wrinkled his nose. "Too dry, girl. Halloween isn't about history."

"So, you're saying we should concentrate on things like being haunted, ghosts, stuff like that?" Hero said slowly.

"Yeah, but what are we supposed to do, come up with our own haunted something or other to report on?" Keera asked.

"I have an idea," Drew interjected. "Let's air the show at midnight, live, on Halloween night. That might add a little excitement to the whole thing."

Amanda's eyes lit up. "Drew, you have a truly brilliant mind," she said, giving him a dazzling smile.

"Thank you," Drew said. "But what did I say?"

"You just gave me the greatest idea. Let's do the show as a finale to the Haunted Homecoming Dance. We can broadcast from Cliffside Bluff, and we can do something on the Legend of Cliffside Bluff," Amanda said.

"What Legend of Cliffside Bluff?" Hero asked. Being a relative newcomer to Cliffside, he didn't know anything about this.

"Oh, Amanda, not that old story," Keera said dismissively.

"Wait a minute, Keera," Jamar said. "With a little hype, that spooky old legend could be okay. We could even have some fun with it."

"Will somebody clue me in here?" Hero asked.

"Anybody else want to tell it?" Amanda asked, looking around at Drew, Keera, and Jamar.

"Amanda, you have the floor," Drew said with a flourish and a bow.

"Well, about a hundred years ago, there were these two feuding families, the Wileys and the Hanovers—"

"As in Melissa Hanover?" Hero interrupted.

Caught off guard by Hero's interest in Melissa, Amanda gave him a sidelong glance and curtly answered, "Yes. Don't interrupt."

"Excuse me," Hero remarked.

"As I was saying," Amanda began again, "these two families really hated each other—like the Montagues and the Capulets in Shakespeare's *Romeo and Juliet*."

"Hey, girl. Don't say the S-man word. That's enough to give me the chills. I haven't done a single English assignment this year," Jamar groaned in a tone of mock distress.

Everyone ignored him. Amanda continued.

"Anyway, the Wileys and the Hanovers were always fighting with each other. They had duels and shoot-outs. The families were business rivals, too. They each owned sheep and cattle ranches and were forever disputing boundaries and who owned the animals," Amanda said.

"Sounds like serious animosity," Hero agreed. "So when do the star-crossed lovers come into this scene? I assume that's what you're leading up to, isn't it?"

"Have you already heard this story?" Amanda asked.

"No, but I *have* read *Romeo and Juliet*," Hero said, smiling, as he nudged Jamar. "Guessed right, didn't I?"

"Do you want to tell it then?" Amanda asked stiffly.

"Amanda, we're not going to beg. Just tell the story," Keera said impatiently.

"Okay, okay. So, of course, against everyone's wishes, Mariah Wiley, the eldest Wiley daughter, and Winston Hanover, the youngest Hanover son, fell in love. Since seeing each other openly was totally out of the question, Mariah and Winston would meet secretly, in the thicket on Cliffside Bluff—you know, Hero, where we used to go during the summer," Amanda reminded Hero with a shy smile.

Hero smiled back, remembering those days when he and Amanda would lie together on the Bluff, the sun streaming through the trees, warm on their faces and backs, as they gazed out over the ocean and held each other for hours. Hero could almost smell the sea water and the vanilla-scented suntan oil that Amanda had worn as he held her in the circle of his arms.

It was a moment before Hero could refocus on Amanda's story.

"So, one Halloween, Mariah and Winston agreed to slip away from the town costume ball and meet at midnight so they could—"

"—elope," Hero finished Amanda's sentence.

"Are you sure you don't know this story?" Amanda asked again.

"Yeah, I lived it in a past life," Hero joked. "Of course, I've never heard this story—it was just obvious. So go ahead, what happened?" Hero asked.

"Nobody really knows. Some people say that someone in either the Wiley or Hanover family found out about the elopement and tried to keep Mariah and Winston from meeting that night at midnight."

"As a result, they each thought the other wasn't coming." Keera picked up the story. "It wasn't until each one heard the other screaming in despair as they leaped over the cliff that they realized they'd both been there the whole time. That's why, on Halloween, you can hear the sounds of screams along the cliff."

"The way I heard it, someone in the Hanover family—or was it the Wiley family—found out about the elopement and came and threw them both over the cliff before they could escape," Jamar said.

"Well, there is another version," Amanda said. "The real one," she added in a hushed voice.

"I didn't know there was a 'real' version," Keera said skeptically.

"Neither did I," Jamar agreed, looking at Amanda curiously.

"Well, the story I know is that one of the Wiley cousins, Jess Wiley, found out about Mariah and Winston's plans to elope from a spiteful Hanover cousin, Clarissa Hanover. She had a crush on Winston and used to follow him around night and day. She happily pointed Jess in the right direction at the Bluff, hoping that something evil would happen.

"Sure enough, things got really scary. By the time Jess arrived at Cliffside Bluff, Mariah and Winston were already there. But instead of lovemaking, like Jess expected, they were arguing. Mariah was pulling away from Winston, who was trying to force her over the cliff.

"Seeing Mariah in danger, Jess jumped off his horse and raced over, hoping to save her. Instead, she slipped from Winston's grasp, and Jess stood frozen while Mariah fell to her death. Angrily, he turned to Winston and they began to fight. Jess probably did want to kill Winston in the beginning. But during the fight, when Winston fell over the cliff, Jess claimed he tried to grab onto him. But Winston was too heavy. He fell onto the rocks, screaming, smashed to pieces.

"Jess Wiley sat at the edge of the cliff, Mariah's and Winston's screams ringing in his ears. He sobbed and sobbed until one of the other Wileys found him there. The Hanovers were furious. They were convinced that Jess had killed both Winston and Mariah, and they wouldn't rest until justice was done. Finally Jess was hanged in the town square on Thanksgiving Day."

"Oooooh." Keera shuddered, a chill running up and down her spine. "But there's one thing I don't get. Why was Winston trying to force Mariah over the cliff?"

"Well, my mother had heard something about Jess and Mariah being in love. Maybe Mariah was trying to break up with Winston that Halloween night, not elope with him."

"You're kidding!" Keera replied. "You mean, Winston killed Mariah because she was trying to leave him?"

Amanda shrugged. "I don't know. No one knows for sure. The only thing we do know is that, if you listen really closely, you can still hear Jess Wiley's sobs along with Mariah and Winston's screams.

"Of course, there's one more thing," Amanda said, looking around the group. "Anyone who gets too close to the cliff at midnight just might end up over the edge—because legend has it that some uneasy evil spirit roams the Bluff on Halloween night, keeping watch to make sure that no one ever learns the whole truth about what went on that horrible night in 1894."

# Chapter Four

*E*veryone in the station was silent.

"Come off it, Amanda," Hero said at last. "That's a wild story—screams, sobs, and now a spirit that haunts the Bluff! Where did you get all that stuff?"

"For your information, Hero, my mother's a Wiley, and that's the story she heard from her great-grandmother," Amanda said haughtily. "Since you've never been up on the Bluff at Halloween, you don't even know what you're talking about," she added.

"You mean, people really believe there are screams and sobs up there?" Hero asked incredulously.

"Anyone who's ever been up on Cliffside Bluff on Halloween does," Amanda retorted.

"Then let's cover the screams at midnight," Hero challenged.

"Cool," Jamar said, sitting upright.

Keera shuddered involuntarily. For some reason, Amanda's story made the thought of filming a show on Cliffside Bluff at midnight seem even more chilling.

"So, Drew. What do you think?" Amanda asked.

"Do it," Drew agreed. "Matter settled. Go forth and create, right now," Drew told them with a smile as he shooed everyone out of his office.

"Slave driver," Amanda grumbled good-naturedly as everyone filed out.

"So, what's our handle on this?" Hero asked as they all sat around at their desks in the main office area.

"I'm thinking spooky music playing throughout, except at midnight, when we're hearing the screams," Jamar said with a grin.

"Cool, but I mean what are we going to do for the hour of air time *before* the screams?" Hero asked.

"I think we need to do some background on this story, maybe go back and read some old newspaper accounts, something like that . . ." Keera volunteered.

"Yeah, but we need an angle," Hero insisted. "We can't just twiddle our thumbs waiting for screams that may or may not happen."

"We could re-enact the legend," Amanda said.

"You mean, stage one of the stories?" Jamar asked with interest.

"Amanda, that is so excellent," Keera said, her eyes sparkling with enthusiasm.

"Not bad," Hero said, nodding his head thoughtfully in approval. "Depending upon what Keera's research turns up, we can act out the most complete or spookiest of the accounts—and then end the show with the screams and sobs.

"But the screams and the sobs have to be real," Hero insisted. "If they really happen, great. If not, then we've debunked the whole legend."

"Agreed," Amanda said, confident that the screams would happen.

"Who should we get to act out the stories?" Jamar asked.

"Why don't we do it ourselves?" Amanda suggested.

"Who—us? Act?" Jamar asked with surprise.

"Definitely. Either Keera or I can play Mariah, Hero can be Winston, and Jamar can be Jess," Amanda said. "We can write the script pretty easily, don't you think, Keera?" Amanda asked, turning to Keera.

"Sure. But if it's all the same with you, I'd rather be the narrator than one of the actors," Keera said, somewhat ill at ease at the thought of being in a love triangle, even if it was only a re-enactment.

"Sure, that's fine," Amanda said agreeably. "I bet my mother even has some old tintypes of Mariah up in the attic somewhere, and tons of clothes from ages ago. I'll dress up to look as much like Mariah as possible."

"Who's going to play the snitch?" Hero asked.

"What do you mean?" Amanda asked.

"Clarissa Hanover. Who's going to set Jess off in the right direction?" Hero wanted to know.

"Oh, we can have that happen off-camera or something. Or maybe Jess can just mutter something about Clarissa," Amanda remarked. "Why, what do you suggest?"

"Why don't we ask an actual Hanover?" Hero remarked. "We could ask Missy Hanover to play Clarissa. That way the whole Wiley/Hanover thing becomes even more authentic, with you as Mariah and Missy as Clarissa."

There was a long silence. Millions of doubts crowded Amanda's mind. What was Hero up to? Why did he want to bring Missy into this? KSS-TV was their own special world—was he trying to get back at Amanda for including Tyler and Samantha in it this summer? Or was he really interested in Melissa?

"Sure, okay. That might work out to be pretty interesting after all," Amanda said slowly, trying not to sound suspicious.

"Great. We can talk to her about it after Keera's done with her research," Hero said, making a note on his pad.

Over my dead body, Amanda thought grimly to herself. There had to be a way to keep Missy Hanover away from KSS—and, more importantly, away from Hero!

# *Chapter Five*

*S*everal days later, Keera was sitting in the library at school, staring at the microfiche machine and reading through articles in the *Cliffside Daily*.

October 30, 1894
As Cliffside gets ready for the town's annual Halloween Costume Ball, the feuding between the Hanovers and the Wileys never ceases. This year, the newly arrived town marshal has announced there will be no gunfighting, street brawling, or any kind of roughhousing permitted on Halloween night, even if that means that all the Wileys and the Hanovers need to be locked up for the whole night. "Things are scary enough on

Halloween without folks stirring things up," the marshal says. "The law runs this town, not the Hanovers and the Wileys. And the law will prevail."

When approached by this reporter for a response to the new marshal's comments, the Hanovers and the Wileys would only say that the marshal was new in town and didn't know how things were run here.

November 1, 1894

This morning, Jess Wiley was taken into custody by the town marshal, over the angry protests of the Wiley family of T-Bone Ranch.

Wiley is charged with the murders of Mariah Wiley and Winston Hanover.

When this reporter asked Jess if he had anything to say for himself, the boy was too overcome with grief over the death of Mariah Wiley to talk. He had been crying since midnight.

It seems odd for a boy to be so broken up about the death of a cousin. Perhaps there's more to this grisly tale of death and murder on Halloween night than we know. But, for now, nobody from the Hanover or the Wiley family is talking.

November 13, 1894

Things are moving quickly on the Wiley/Hanover murder trial, now that the prosecution has found a surprise eyewitness.

It seems that fourteen-year-old Clarissa Hanover happened to be hiding in a thicket on Cliffside Bluff on Halloween night. She claims to have seen Jess Wiley throw first Mariah Wiley and then Winston Hanover over the cliff.

Nobody knows what took Clarissa so long to come forward or what she was doing out on the Bluff so late that night. But with Clarissa as an eyewitness, it seems as though

Jess's hanging is a foregone conclusion.

There doesn't seem to be anybody in town who believes Jess's story about Winston pushing Mariah off the cliff and Jess accidentally pushing Winston down after her.

Jess also claims that Clarissa Hanover framed him and that the whole murder plot was something Clarissa Hanover dreamed up. But nobody believes a word of that. It seems that a desperate man will say anything to save his own skin.

As Keera read, her eyes widened as she realized that, without Clarissa Hanover, there might not have been a case against Jess Wiley. Wait till Amanda hears this, Keera thought to herself.

While Keera pondered this piece of information, she felt a presence hovering above her. Looking up, Keera found herself staring straight into the dark, laughing eyes of Jordan Harris, who was leaning over Keera's microfiche machine and gazing intently into her face.

"Hey, Keera. What are you up to?" Jordan asked easily, pulling up a chair.

"Oh, I'm just doing some research for the KSS show we're working up for Halloween," Keera replied, aware of how close Jordan's arm was to her own.

Whistling in admiration, Jordan said ruefully, "I can't believe that you've got time to do extra research. I've barely got it together enough to do the work I have to do."

Blushing slightly, Keera ducked her head toward the screen. After making a quick note of the entry, she shut down the machine.

"Hey, I didn't mean to interrupt you," Jordan said. "Go ahead, I'll wait till you're done."

"That's okay. I found out some really interesting stuff," Keera said.

Jordan stared admiringly at Keera. "You're the girl with everything: good grades, good looks, great job. How do you do it, girl?" Jordan asked.

Embarrassed to speechlessness, Keera was grateful when the bell rang. Jordan moved back slightly, scraping his chair along the floor to allow Keera to get up as well. They both stood up at the same time, their arms brushing against each other.

Keera tried to calm the thumping in her chest as her skin tingled at the touch of Jordan's arm against hers. For a moment, Jordan didn't move back, and Keera didn't know which way to look.

Swallowing hard, trying to keep her heart from leaping out of her throat, Keera responded in what she hoped was a nonchalant tone.

"Oh, you're not so shabby yourself, you know—basketball superstar, girls following you everywhere. I'll bet all the really great colleges are falling all over themselves to recruit you."

A shadow crossed Jordan's face.

"That's the problem. All the colleges want to recruit me, but my grades just aren't there—yet," Jordan said. "But I'm working on it," he added brightly.

"Well, I better be going before I'm

late," Keera said, glancing up at the clock over the library door.

"Meeting someone?" Jordan asked casually as he fell into step alongside Keera.

"No, actually, I'm going to chem class," Keera said.

"I see. Well, then," Jordan said, clearing his throat nervously.

"See you around, Jordan," Keera said, turning the corner at the end of the hall.

"Uh, Keera. Maybe we can, uh, get together sometime—and talk some more," Jordan called after her.

Keera could hardly believe her ears. She was afraid to look back and face Jordan. She didn't want him to see how excited she was.

"Sure, that would be great," Keera called over her shoulder, making a bee line for her chem class.

Keera sat down in class in a daze. There was no way she could keep her mind on what the teacher was saying. Instead, she found herself drifting off, riding beside Jordan in his convertible, Jordan's arm around her shoulders, her hair blowing in the wind, Jordan's face moving closer and closer to hers, their lips barely touching . . .

"Ahem, Ms. Johnson. Would you care to enlighten us on the physical properties of $H_2C_2$ combined with $CO_2$?" Mr. Wainscot, the chemistry teacher, asked.

"Uh, sure, Mr. Wainscot, one minute," Keera said, flipping through her notes, trying to regain her composure.

There was a long silence.

"Perhaps the next time I call on you, you'll be more prepared, Ms. Johnson. This really isn't like you," the teacher commented drily, moving on to the next student.

This is just great, Keera thought to herself. I haven't been this dizzy since I first started seeing Jamar.

Keera bit her lip at the thought of Jamar and how disloyal she was to even think about Jordan Harris. Keera vowed to put all thoughts of Jordan Harris out of her mind. But every time Keera attempted to focus on the symbols on the periodic chart, she could only see Jordan's face in front of her.

If I'm going to be goofing off in chemistry, I should be thinking about Jamar, Keera scolded herself. Instead, she thought about what it would be like to kiss Jordan Harris. She hoped that Jordan Harris was thinking the very same thing.

# Chapter Six

The next day, Keera spotted Amanda racing down the hall on her way to lunch. "Amanda!" Keera called, breaking into a trot. "Wait up. I've got to talk to you."

"Oh, Keera. I'm sorry I didn't get back to you last night after you called," Amanda apologized as Keera fell into step beside her. "But the planning committee met really late, and then Hero called, and I had so much homework that I practically fell asleep over my books. My sister, Kit, said you had something important to tell me. What was it?"

"It's about the Bluff legend. I was reading some of the articles from the Cliffside paper back then. Remember how you said Clarissa Hanover told Jess Wiley where Mariah and Winston were going to meet? Well, it turns out she was also an eyewitness to the murder. She actually *saw* Jess Wiley push Mariah and Winston over the edge."

"What?" Amanda said, standing completely still. "Is that really what the paper said?"

"Uh-huh," Keera responded, nodding her head. "So I guess part of your story is true, anyway. But it looks as though Jess Wiley really was guilty."

"I wonder about that," Amanda said thoughtfully. "But now we will need someone to play Clarissa for the re-enactment," she added, looking straight at Keera.

"Don't look at me," Keera said, shaking her head. "I'm the narrator, remember?"

"Okay, I'm sure we'll think of something," Amanda said. "Anyway, Keera, we need to get together and work on the script, if all your research is done. How about tomorrow night—unless you're busy with Jamar?" Amanda asked.

"Busy with Jamar? Surely you're

joking. That boy is on a never-ending music gig. He's so busy preparing for the Torch Club gig and, now, writing the Halloween show music, I may never see him again," Keera said drily. "Tomorrow night sounds fine. Now let's go eat. I'm starved," Keera added.

"You go ahead. I forgot I was supposed to take care of something for the planning committee. Tell Hero I'll be down in a few minutes," Amanda said over her shoulder as she hurried back down the hall.

As Keera entered the spacious lunchroom of Cliffside High, her eyes roamed over the bright turquoise tables lined up throughout the room, searching for Hero and Jamar. Spotting Hero off in a quiet corner, Keera went over and touched him lightly on the shoulder of his leather jacket.

"Hey, Keera. Have a seat," Hero said, moving a chair out for her.

"Thanks," Keera said, sitting down and dropping her books and lunch bag on the table.

"Have you seen Amanda?" Hero

asked. "She was supposed to be meeting me here, but, as usual, she's late."

"She said to tell you she'd be right here. She just had some planning committee stuff to do," Keera said.

Keera noticed Hero's grimace at the words "planning committee." It was the same way she felt about the word "JellyJam."

Flashing Hero a sympathetic smile, Keera said, "Guess what? Yesterday, I found out some interesting stuff about the legend."

She quickly filled Hero in about Clarissa Hanover being an eyewitness to the murders. "She's why Jess Wiley was hanged. So Amanda and I were thinking we probably do need to have someone play Clarissa Hanover for the show after all," Keera added before heading up to the lunch counter to get something to drink.

Hero's eyes opened wide. If Keera had read actual news accounts of the story, then at least some of what went on at Cliffside Bluff on Halloween might actually be true. Usually Hero didn't believe in ghost stories, but this one was beginning to get a hold on him.

Deep in thought, Hero was interrupted as a cool hand playfully smoothed back his hair from his forehead. Expecting Amanda, Hero reached back without looking and encircled the person behind him with his strong hands, pulling her body toward his and leaning his head back for a kiss. But in the next moment, he realized that the soft, clinging sweater under his fingers didn't feel like Amanda.

Surprised, Hero looked up and saw that he had Missy Hanover in his arms.

"Hey, there. Nice greeting. I'm happy to see you, too," Missy remarked with a mischievous smile, touching her lips lightly to Hero's.

Immediately, Hero let go of her, as though he had touched fire. His lips burned from Missy's soft kiss. Flushing darkly, Hero said, "Sorry, Missy. I was expecting . . . "

"Amanda. I know." Missy finished

the sentence for him. Then, shaking her head, she said, "That girl just doesn't know how lucky she is. Well, I enjoyed the moment while it lasted," Missy said with a mock sigh. Then, pointing to the seat next to Hero, Missy asked, "Is anybody sitting there, or is it reserved?"

"No. I mean, yes. I mean, sure, go ahead and sit down," Hero answered, feeling a little flustered.

"So where is the committee queen this time?" Missy remarked, as she set down her tray and pulled her chair up close to Hero's.

"Amanda? She'll be here . . . any day now," Hero replied with a good-natured grin. He looked quickly around the room to see if Amanda was, in fact, anywhere in sight, half-hoping that she was not.

Then Hero turned his attention back to Missy. It was hard not to pay attention to her. Her cat-green eyes gazed directly into Hero's dark brown eyes. Her perfect bow-shaped mouth sipped seductively on a straw, while a tiny smile played around her lips.

"Well, then, I guess I'll have to make

the most of the time I have with you alone," Missy said.

Hero's heart raced. Missy Hanover, Homecoming Queen, wanted to spend time alone with him. Hero couldn't quite get over it.

"Where's Tyler?" Hero asked pointedly.

"Oh, he's around, I suppose," Missy answered with a careless wave of her hand. "Let's not waste time talking about Tyler. What's up with you? Working on a Halloween TV special, I hear..."

"Yeah. We've worked out a pretty good handle for this one, I think," Hero began to say.

"I think the shows you've been doing have been really wonderful, Hero. Your segments especially," Missy remarked, touching Hero lightly on the arm as she spoke.

"Thanks," Hero said, enjoying the tingling feeling that ran through him at Missy's touch.

"So, what's the handle for this show?" Missy asked, never taking her eyes from Hero's face.

"Actually, it's something you might be interested in," Hero remarked. "We're doing a re-enactment of the Legend of Cliffside Bluff."

"Hmmmm," Missy said, moving in just a bit closer to Hero. "What's that all about?"

"You mean you don't know?" Hero asked, incredulous.

"Not really," Missy replied. "I don't really pay attention to local lore stuff."

"I would have thought you'd know all about it. It's about your family—you know, the feuding between the Hanovers and the Wileys, the murders on the Bluff," Hero said.

"Oh, that old stuff. My parents used to tell us that story when we were kids. You don't actually believe in that old legend with the screams and the sobs, do you?"

"Well, I don't know about the screams and the sobs," Hero said slowly, not wanting Missy to think he was immature. "But Keera Johnson was doing some research in the newspapers from 1894, and the deaths on the Bluff really did happen. In fact, it turns out there was an eyewitness to the murders. Someone from your family—Clarissa Hanover."

"Really?" Missy asked. She didn't seem particularly interested as Hero briefly gave her the details of the legend and the plans to re-enact the story.

"So do you think you might be interested in playing Clarissa?" Hero asked.

Just then Keera returned to the table with Amanda. Missy smiled cattily at Amanda and moved her chair closer toward Hero to make room for the girls to sit down.

"Hey, you," Amanda said, swinging past Missy to brush Hero's lips with her own. Hero caught her hand in his, looking deep into her eyes.

"Hey, you, glad you could make it," Hero said teasingly.

"Thanks," Amanda said in a tight voice. Then she made a point of sitting on the other side of the table, across from Hero and next to Keera.

"So, what were we just talking about, Hero?" Missy turned to Hero, all sweetness and attention.

"I thought since Clarissa Hanover is your ancestor, you might be interested in playing her part in the Halloween show," Hero said.

Amanda let out a long breath and her face went pale. I can't believe Hero is doing this, she thought.

Missy glanced over at Amanda. Noting her unhappy expression, she turned back to Hero and said warmly, "Why, I'd love to play the part of Clarissa"

"Great," Hero said, happy he had solved the problem of finding someone to play the part.

"Oh, but you'll be so busy during the Haunted Halloween Dance with all the Homecoming Queen stuff, you won't have time to come up to the Bluff to do the show live, will you?" Amanda asked with false concern.

"Well, you can surely fix that, can't you, Amanda?" Missy said. "I mean, let's just move up the homecoming ceremonies to the middle of the dance, instead of at the end, and then I'll be able to come up to the Bluff with you."

"That's a great idea. What's the point

of having an in with the planning committee if you can't get things done the way you want them?" Hero asked.

Missy smiled at Hero and touched him on the shoulder. "Isn't he just the cutest thing?"

Amanda's face flushed. "He's simply adorable," she said grimly, with an expression that meant he was anything but.

Scanning the crowded cafeteria, Missy got up and said coyly, "I've got to run, Hero. Call me and let me know what you want me to do and when. I'll be ready, anywhere, anytime."

"Great. We'll do that," Hero said, blushing.

The second Missy left the table, silence descended upon the group. Looking anxiously from Amanda to Hero and back again, Keera decided it was absolutely imperative that she go to her locker that very minute.

As Keera got up to leave, Jamar came up behind her. Practically lifting her off her feet, Jamar gave Keera a huge hug and whirled her around so he could kiss her.

"Hey, Jamar. Good to see you," Hero said, grateful for Jamar's sudden interruption.

"Hey, dude. Hand me five!" Jamar said, slapping Hero's hand hard. "Hey, Amanda. What's up?" Not waiting for an answer, Jamar turned eagerly to Keera.

"Girlfriend, where have you been?" Jamar asked.

"Around," Keera said. "What are you doing here? Don't tell me you've finally decided to go to classes."

"Hey, no way. But I'm always up for lunch," Jamar said with a grin. "No, seriously, my guidance counselor told me if I don't start going to classes, she's going to tell my mom I shouldn't be working at KSS. So, here I am."

"Well, I was just about to go," Keera said, not finding anything Jamar had to say amusing today. The contrast between Jordan Harris, who was trying desperately to keep up with class, and Jamar, who did everything but go to class, was weighing heavily on Keera's mind.

"Then so was I," Jamar said with a

grin, slouching out of the cafeteria at Keera's side.

The bell rang and the cafeteria started to empty out. Missy Hanover made a point of waving to Hero as she exited.

"I've got trig next," Hero said. "Come on, I'll walk you to your next class."

"No need. I can get there on my own. But you might want to ask Missy if she needs help finding her next class," Amanda said snidely.

"Look, Amanda, is Missy what you're so upset about?" Hero asked.

"Upset? Who's upset?" Amanda asked, hoping her voice didn't sound too shrill.

"Look, Amanda, if this is about Missy being in the show, I just thought I was helping out. Keera told me we needed someone to play Clarissa, and Missy seemed like the perfect choice. But if you don't want her in the show, let's forget it. We'll get someone else, or we won't have anyone," Hero said, trying to make things right.

Seeing how contrite Hero looked, Amanda calmed down. It wasn't Hero's fault that Missy was hanging all over him, although he wasn't exactly stopping her.

"Come on, Amanda. Let's get going," Hero urged, putting his arm possessively around Amanda's shoulders.

Amanda looked into Hero's eyes. He looked so sincere, Amanda gave in.

"Okay. I'm sorry, Hero," Amanda told him as they started walking toward Amanda's English class. "It'll be fine with Missy playing Clarissa. In fact, it will be perfect. After all, having real descendants of the Hanovers and Wileys doing the show will make it seem more real and even spookier." Amanda's eyes began to sparkle. "In fact, we'll play up that whole angle in the intro. I'll talk to Keera about it." Amanda gave Hero a slightly distracted kiss on the mouth, then dashed into class.

As Hero walked toward trig class, he couldn't get Missy Hanover out of his head. His hands still tingled from touching her. And her cat-green eyes seemed to be shining out at him from everywhere he looked.

Hero had thought he meant it when he told Amanda he loved her. But now, with Missy in the picture, Hero wasn't so sure.

# Chapter Seven

𝒥or the next several days, Missy and Hero always seemed to be in the same place at the same time. Amanda, meanwhile, was spending lots of time with Tyler on the planning committee.

"So, what's doing with your Halloween TV special?" Tyler asked Amanda, walking her to her car after the latest committee meeting.

"Keera and I are just about finished with the script, and we have all of next week to learn the lines and rough out the staging before the big night," Amanda told him.

"Sounds like a lot of work for you," Tyler said sympathetically. "Anything I can do to help?"

"Thanks, Tyler. You've already been such a big help to me with this committee stuff . . . and I don't really think it's a good idea for you to be involved in any KSS projects," Amanda said.

"Yeah, I guess Hero and Drew are still sore about that prank I pulled on the computer. I just wanted to see if I could pull it off. I didn't really mean to do you or Hero or anyone at the station any real harm. You believe me, don't you Amanda?"

"I know, Tyler. Really, it's fine. I've forgiven you, and I'm sure that someday Hero will, too," Amanda said, patting Tyler gently on the arm.

Tyler covered Amanda's hand with his own and looked deeply into her eyes. "You know, I really would do anything for you, Amanda," Tyler said softly.

Feeling Tyler's warm hand on her own, Amanda looked back into Tyler's eyes. There were no suspicions there, no complaints. Tyler was just looking at her, willing to do anything she asked.

Amanda sighed to herself. If only Hero could be a little more like Tyler about this kind of stuff.

Tyler sensed Amanda's interest and

started to move closer. He bent his head, intent upon kissing Amanda.

Startled, Amanda stepped back, breaking the mood.

For a minute, Tyler's eyes iced over and his lips tightened. But then he relaxed, refusing to allow anything Amanda did or said to make him angry in front of her.

"Missy Hanover tells me that Hero asked her to be in the show. I was kind of surprised to hear that," Tyler said as they continued along the path to the parking lot.

"Yes. I wasn't too crazy about the idea at first," Amanda said. "But when I thought about it, what Hero had said made sense. Having a real Hanover and a real Wiley in the show makes it seem more authentic."

"I guess that explains why Missy and Hero have been spending so much time together," Tyler commented.

"What do you mean?"

"Oh, you know, motorcycle rides down by the beach, afternoon meetings at the Bluff, stuff like that," Tyler said casually.

Amanda's cheeks stained red. She felt like she'd been punched in the stomach. Hero had taken Missy for rides on his motorcycle? And he'd taken her to the Bluff? When had all this happened? And how could Amanda not have noticed it?

"How do you know what Missy and Hero have been doing?" Amanda asked, suddenly suspicious.

"Missy told me, how else?" Tyler said. "I'm sorry, Amanda. I thought you knew."

"Knew what?" Amanda said. She suddenly remembered that Hero hadn't called her for the past few days and that he'd been kind of distant at the latest KSS meetings.

"Nothing. Forget I mentioned it," Tyler said, putting his arm around Amanda as they got to his car. "Hey, I've got a great idea. Let's go for a ride ourselves. I've been wanting to let the Porsche loose on the road. I can pick you up tomorrow morning, so you don't have to come back for your car today."

Amanda could hardly focus on what

Tyler was saying, she was so distracted by the thought of Missy and Hero together on his cycle and together at the Bluff. "Sure, that'd be great," she mumbled.

After opening the car door for Amanda, Tyler strolled around to the driver's side and put down the top. Then, without warning, he tore out of the Cliffside High parking lot with a neck-breaking jolt.

But Amanda didn't complain. The image of Hero with Missy kept floating before her eyes, so real that Amanda almost imagined she saw them together, watching her tear out of the parking lot in Tyler's car.

Mrs. Townsend hurried to open the door when Tyler rang the bell of the Townsend house the next morning.

"Tyler, how good to see you. Amanda told me you'd be picking her up this morning, and I just wanted to say hello," Mrs. Townsend said in the friendly voice she reserved for her circle of friends at the Yacht Club, but for no one else.

"Good morning, Mrs. Townsend. You're looking lovely, as always," Tyler said ingratiatingly.

"Why, thank you, Tyler. You always know just the right thing to say to a girl," Mrs. Townsend tittered.

Amanda, overhearing their conversation, was annoyed at how sweet Mrs. Townsend was being to Tyler. It was quite a contrast to the stone-cold silences with which she greeted Hero.

Slipping past her mother, Amanda called good-bye and practically dragged Tyler toward the car and away from her house.

"Hey, not so fast," Tyler said. "I was hoping for a little show of affection. How about a kiss?" Tyler moved closer to Amanda, drawing her body toward him.

Amanda hesitated. Tyler had been very sweet to her lately, helping her on the planning committee and listening to her talk about all the things she had to do. In fact, he'd been a lot better to her these last few days than Hero had been.

And it wasn't like Tyler was gross or

unappealing. Half the girls in school would kill to have Tyler Scott kiss them—Samantha Walker, Amanda's former best friend, included.

Amanda gazed into Tyler's clear, blue eyes. Maybe she could get used to thinking of Tyler as something more than just a friend. Maybe . . .

At that moment, the image of Hero riding along the beach with Missy Hanover on the back of his cycle floated into Amanda's head.

Forget maybe. Amanda put one hand behind Tyler's head and gently pulled his mouth down to hers. Tyler quickly encircled Amanda with his arms, pressing his lips urgently against hers as his hands traveled the length of her slim back.

Suddenly confused, Amanda pulled away from Tyler's embrace. "What are we doing?" she said. "Come on, Tyler. Not now. We'll be late for class."

"Not now? Then when?" Tyler asked in a low, hoarse voice.

Amanda didn't answer. Briefly, she thought of Hero. But then Tyler's face crowded Hero's image from her mind.

Was she really finding Tyler attractive? Or was she just jealous of Hero and Missy?

Whatever it was, things were moving too fast for her. Amanda needed some time alone to think about what she was feeling. More importantly, she needed to talk to Hero.

"Let's plan on taking a drive after school," Tyler said as he opened the door for Amanda and she got in. But Amanda said nothing. They drove in silence toward school, both lost in their own thoughts.

Tyler's car roared into the parking lot at school and stopped with a screech. Tyler quickly hopped out to open the door for Amanda.

"Thanks for the ride, Tyler. I really appreciate it," Amanda said, suddenly shy. She moved quickly past Tyler toward the school building.

"Hey, not so fast," Tyler said meaningfully, holding Amanda's arm tightly to keep her from leaving his side.

Amanda searched Tyler's face. Impulsively, she stroked his jawline with one finger, hoping that the touch of her skin on his would have the same tingling effect on her as touching Hero did.

Tyler bent down. Once again, he hungrily sought Amanda's lips with his own. Amanda waited for rockets to explode.

But there was nothing.

Stepping back, Amanda held Tyler at arm's length. "Tyler, I . . ."

That's when Amanda saw Hero, watching her with Tyler, his fists clenched at his sides, his eyes flaming.

It was the longest moment of Amanda's life. Frozen in dismay beside Tyler, she looked helplessly over at Hero.

Just then the bell rang. Sounds and movement came back in with a rush, crashing against Amanda's ears and filling her brain with confusion.

In that moment, Hero wheeled around and stormed through the school doorway, mingling with the throng of other students on their way to class.

Tyler, following Amanda's gaze,

turned around just in time to see Hero disappear from sight. Looking back at Amanda, Tyler's eyes narrowed with pleasure.

"I'll pick you up after your last class," Tyler said, possessively placing his hand on Amanda's shoulder.

"Yeah, I'll see you, Tyler," Amanda said, distracted, as she took off after Hero.

Tyler grinned. Everything was going perfectly according to plan. He had Amanda and Hero right where he wanted them. And this time he wasn't going to make any mistakes.

# Chapter Eight

$B$y the time Amanda caught up to Hero, he was deeply engrossed in a conversation with none other than Missy Hanover. Amanda hesitated, watching Missy throw back her head and laugh as she stood within the circle of Hero's arm where it leaned against his locker.

Hero tried to keep his attention solely on Missy. But his eyes flickered toward Amanda when he saw her approaching.

Following Hero's brief glance, Missy stiffened slightly. Arching her back and moving her body closer to Hero's, she fixed her eyes on Hero's mouth as if to concentrate on what he was saying.

Hero shifted uncomfortably at the intensity of Missy's gaze. He definitely enjoyed her attention, but sometimes he wondered just what was going on behind those cat-green eyes of hers. The mystery both repelled and excited him.

Whenever Hero looked into Amanda's clear violet eyes, he immediately knew what she was thinking or feeling. That had been one of the things he loved best about her.

Amanda cleared her throat loudly as she walked up to where Hero and Missy were lounging.

"Oh, Mandy. How nice to see you," Missy said with forced cheer. "We were just talking about you and Tyler, weren't we, Hero?" She moved so close to Hero that the loose ends of her rich, auburn hair tickled his chin.

Amanda blushed to the roots of her blonde hair. Determined to ignore Missy, she looked straight at Hero. "I really think we need to talk," she told him.

Hero's jaw stiffened. He refused to meet Amanda's gaze, but Amanda stood her ground, waiting.

Looking from Amanda to Hero, Missy sighed deeply and said, "Guess

I'll be running along to class. See you later, Hero."

Hero forced his mouth into a smile, which he directed at Missy. But his eyes remained anything but smiling, as they gazed stonily at Amanda.

"Bye, Mandy," Missy called over her shoulder with a hint of derision.

"Mandy?" Hero said, with a question in his eyes.

"Don't call me thàt, please. I hate that nickname, and Missy knows it," Amanda said in a low voice.

"Missy seems to know an awful lot about you," Hero commented.

"What's that supposed to mean?" Amanda asked.

"Well, she's been telling me how friendly you and Tyler have become. Of course, I saw that for myself in the parking lot," Hero said. His stomach churned at the memory of Tyler with his arms around Amanda.

"Hero, I can explain . . . that was all a mis—" Amanda began to say.

"Please, spare me the explanations," Hero interrupted. "I could see for myself what was going on. I don't

85

have to belong to a fancy Yacht Club or wear a letter sweater to figure it out."

Amanda's eyes crackled with anger.

"I suppose there's nothing going on between you and Missy Hanover? I've heard all about the two of you, too," Amanda fired back.

"I don't know what you're talking about," Hero said.

"Really? That's not what I've heard," Amanda snapped.

"And who have you heard it from—Tyler?" Hero asked, his eyes narrowed to slits. "No, don't tell me. It doesn't matter. It's pretty clear who you'd rather spend your time with. If I've been spending time with Missy Hanover, it's because she wants to spend time with *me*! She's not running around doing planning committee stuff or a thousand other things that seem to be so much more important than I am," Hero said angrily.

"Thanks for all the helpful support," Amanda retorted.

"You don't need my support. You seem to prefer Tyler's," Hero remarked.

Tears stung Amanda's eyes at the bitterness in Hero's voice. He wouldn't even let her explain.

"Maybe you're right," Amanda said, her hands trembling as she spoke. "Maybe . . . maybe, we should let it go for a while."

In stunned silence, Hero listened as Amanda's words shattered his heart.

"I think it might be for the best. And I think you think so, too," Amanda said in a shaky voice, filling the silence with more words. "So, I guess this is it, then."

"Amanda . . . wait," Hero began. But the bell rang loudly above them, cutting him off.

"I've got to go, Hero," Amanda said. "I-I-I'll see you around."

And with that, Amanda turned and walked away.

Hero flushed darkly as he stood alone in the hallway, watching Amanda walk out of his life. Students on their way to class hurried past, bumping into him as he strained for a last glimpse of Amanda's figure as it receded into the crowd. How could the world go on around him, when his universe had just ground to a total halt?

Looking down, Hero was surprised to see that he was holding his books in his hands. His arms felt so empty. Already he was missing the feel of Amanda in his arms, the touch of her hair against his face, and her soft, sweet mouth.

A sob tore through Hero's body. Without thinking, he turned around and punched the door of his locker in—hard. Then he stared at his hand, which was already starting to bruise along the knuckles. But he felt nothing except a terrible aching in his chest.

Get a grip on yourself, man, Hero thought. He forced himself to walk to class. By the time Hero arrived, he had regained his composure. But one question ran through his mind, over and over again.

How was he going to face Amanda again, at school and at the station, without feeling like his heart was being ripped apart?

# Chapter Nine

*L*ater that day, Keera was finishing up some last-minute research on the Cliffside Bluff legend before she and Amanda met to finalize the script at Keera's house.

After finding out about some unexplained coincidences surrounding the events on the Bluff, Keera was taking this whole legend a lot more seriously. She had to say, Amanda's belief in the truth behind the legend had a lot more basis in fact than Keera liked to admit.

Leafing through some follow-up articles about Halloween legends in their area, Keera found a long footnote about the Cliffside Bluff legend in a recent issue of *Newsmonth*, a local magazine.

. . . Concerning the mysterious double murder of Mariah Wiley and Winston Hanover, which took place in 1894 at Cliffside Bluff, some startling new evidence has come to light.

A homeowner recently discovered the private journal of Clarissa Hanover, who played a prominent role in the identification and ultimate conviction of Jess Wiley, the man who was found guilty of the murders and who was hanged in the town square.

The journal reveals the very diabolical mind of fourteen-year-old Clarissa Hanover. Clarissa, in love with her cousin Winston, actually orchestrated the sad events of that fateful night, and had plotted them for some time.

Clarissa knew Jess Wiley to be somewhat of a simpleton and also knew of his crush on Mariah. But when Jess refused Clarissa's overtures to try to sabotage Winston and Mariah's love, she decided to take her revenge on them all.

By her own admission, Clarissa told Winston, on the eve of his elopement, that Mariah and Jess were in love, knowing it would enrage him. Then Clarissa made sure that Jess knew where Winston and Mariah would be meeting on Halloween night. She told Jess that Winston intended to elope with Mariah only for her money, asserting that Winston's branch of the Hanover family was in deep financial trouble.

The rest, as they say, is Cliffside history. Perhaps this also explains why Clarissa Hanover threw herself off Cliffside Bluff when she was only twenty-one years old.

Skimming the rest of the article, Keera noted that, since Clarissa's suicide in 1901, there had been several suspicious deaths in that same area.

"Keera, girl, you look like you've

91

just seen a ghost," a voice said, startling her out of her reading. Jordan Harris came up and sat close beside Keera, casually resting his arm right above her shoulders on the back of the library couch.

"More like reading about them," Keera said, making every effort not to blush at Jordan's nearness.

"Doing more research for the show?" Jordan asked with interest.

Keera nodded, eager to share the information she'd learned.

"You'll never believe what I found out. It was Clarissa Hanover all along, just like Amanda thought it was. We all thought she was paranoid or crazy or something, but it was true . . ."

"Whoa, slow down! I don't have a clue what you're talking about. Although I like the way your eyes send out little sparks when you get excited," Jordan said, moving his arm to rest gently on Keera's shoulders.

Keera caught her breath. She looked shyly into Jordan's eyes.

"Keera," Jordan said softly, his face moving closer to hers. "There's something I've really been wanting to ask you."

Keera's stomach tightened. Was Jordan Harris really about to ask her out, here and now? What should she say? What about Jamar? Keera half-closed her eyes, expecting Jordan to bend his head and cover her mouth with his, just as she had been dreaming about for several days.

"Hey, Keera. Girl, where have you been? I've been looking for you." Jamar's voice boomed from across the room.

Heads turned in Keera's direction. Jordan carefully removed his arm from around Keera's shoulders.

"Hey, Jordan. How's it going?" Jamar said, eyeing Jordan suspiciously.

"Hey, Jamar. Well, I'm outta here. Gotta be at the guidance counselor's office in three minutes," Jordan said, hastily getting to his feet. "Catch you later, Keera," he added, lightly tapping Keera's shoulder before heading for the library door.

"You're spending an awful lot of time with that dude," Jamar commented, sitting close beside Keera and looking her straight in the eyes.

"Not really," Keera murmured, lowering her eyes from the scrutiny of Jamar's gaze.

"What were you and he talking about?" Jamar asked casually.

"Just the legend." Keera paused. "Oh, Jamar, you're never going to believe what I found out today, about the legend. Amanda was right, and it's going to make the script so exciting."

"What is it, girl? Tell me before you burst," Jamar said, caught up in Keera's excitement.

Keera told Jamar about the article she'd read. Jamar's eyes widened, and he hung on her every word. When Keera was done explaining, Jamar just whistled.

"Cool. Just wait till Amanda and Hero hear about this," Jamar said. "Keera, you're the best researcher in the universe."

Without hesitation, Keera leaned over and kissed Jamar full on the mouth, a deep, long kiss, just like the one she'd been hoping Jordan would give her.

"What was that all about?" Jamar asked.

"Oh, just because I felt like it," Keera answered.

"I like that," Jamar said, moving in closer for a replay.

"Another time," Keera teased, looking toward the librarian. Ms. Henshaw was glaring at them from across the room.

"What do you mean another time? Come with me, girl," Jamar said, taking Keera's hands and pulling her up from the couch.

"Wait a minute. Let me put these things back," Keera said, laughing as the magazine articles spilled from her lap.

Jamar waited, tapping his hands in an impatient drum roll along the library desks, much to the dismay of the librarian.

The bell shrilled loudly.

"Keera, let's go before that prune-faced witch cuts off our heads," Jamar said, whisking her out of the library door. "So, are we on for Friday night at the Torch Club, and Saturday for the dance?" Jamar asked. He didn't expect Keera to say anything other than "yes" as they walked comfortably arm in arm toward her next class.

For a moment, Keera remembered Jordan's handsome face, bending close in toward hers. "There's something I wanted to ask you" echoed in her ears. Had Jordan been planning to ask her out this weekend?

"Keera?" Jamar asked, turning to look her in the face.

Keera blushed. Determined to put all thoughts of Jordan Harris out of her mind, she replied, "Of course, Friday at the Torch Club, Saturday at the dance." She patted Jamar's cheek. "Now, don't forget, Amanda and I are finishing the script tonight, and we're all supposed to meet on Friday night at seven to practice. We've been planning this for over a week, Jamar," Keera said, "so make sure you remember."

"Time's going to be tight. I have to be at the gig at nine," Jamar said.

Keera looked at him reprovingly.

"No problem, girl. I'll make it," Jamar hurried to reassure her. "And then you all can come see me play after the rehearsal."

"I'll tell Amanda and see what she says."

"Amanda the party girl? She'll be there with bells on." Jamar gave Keera a quick hug and a grin.

"Probably," Keera said cheerfully. "I'll talk to her about it tonight."

# Chapter Ten

Amanda rang Keera's doorbell at seven-thirty that night.

Keera answered the door, anxious to tell Amanda all the news—about Clarissa, about Jess, about Jamar's gig on Friday night. But before Keera could say a word, she noticed that Amanda's eyes were puffy and red.

"Amanda, come on in. What's wrong?" Keera asked with concern, forgetting everything she wanted to say.

"Oh, Keera," Amanda said, drawing a shuddering breath. "This has just been the worst day."

"Hey, Amanda," Keera's younger brother Akim shouted, bouncing into the foyer.

"Hey," Amanda said weakly, trying to pretend nothing was wrong.

Squinting, Akim said, "Gee, Amanda, you look funny."

"Thanks," Amanda answered, her eyes filling again.

"Beat it, small fry," Keera said, swatting at Akim with a newspaper she grabbed off the table. "Amanda, let's go up to my room so we can talk."

"Let's go up to my room so we can talk," Akim mimicked, with all the contempt a seven-year-old brother could muster. "Yakkety-yak, that's all you girls ever do," he added with disgust.

Amanda headed for Keera's room. She threw herself across the worn handmade bedspread that adorned Keera's bed, sighing heavily.

"What's up, Amanda?" Keera asked sympathetically. "Is your mother down on you again? Or is it . . ." Keera left the other possible reason for Amanda's tears hanging in the air.

" . . . Hero? Isn't that what you were going to say?" Amanda said.

Keera nodded.

Amanda took another deep, shaky breath. Tears spilled out of her violet eyes and trickled down her cheeks.

Keera put her arms around Amanda's shoulders, holding her close as Amanda's thin frame shook from the force of her sobs.

"He-He-Hero," Amanda started to say, barely able to say his name, " . . . and I b-b-b-broke up."

"Oh, Amanda. I'm so sorry," Keera murmured. Amanda sounded like her heart was about to break. "What happened?"

Amanda gulped again, reaching for a tissue from the box on the night table by Keera's bed.

"I-I-I don't know. Tyler told me about Hero and that barracuda Missy Hanover. She's been all over Hero the past week or so. And then . . . and then . . . when I asked Hero about it, he got mad at me, and . . . then he saw Tyler and me. But that was all a mistake, but Hero . . . I-I-I said we should break up, and so we did," Amanda said between hiccups.

"Oh, Amanda. I'm so sorry. You must feel awful," Keera said sympathetically. She didn't completely understand the circumstances, but the result was clear enough.

"And what's worse is that it's over Missy Hanover, of all people. I hate Missy Hanover. She was always trying to bully me and take away my things when we were kids. And now—now she's taken away Hero." Amanda sobbed into Keera's shoulder, wetting Keera's shirt with her tears.

Finally, Amanda's sobs subsided. Still hiccuping slightly, she lifted her head, dabbing at Keera's damp shoulder with a clean tissue.

"I guess I really needed a shoulder to cry on," Amanda said with a small smile.

Keera smiled back.

"So," Amanda said, taking a deep breath. "Now that I've told you what a mess my life is, what's new with you?"

"You're a hard act to follow," Keera said with another smile.

"Some people don't think so," Amanda said, her eyes filling again at the thought of Hero with Missy.

Keera quickly changed the subject. "Listen to this," she said, and filled in Amanda on Clarissa Hanover's journal and the recent "accidents" on the Bluff.

By the end of Keera's recounting, Amanda had almost forgotten how sad she was about Hero.

"I knew it," Amanda said, her cheeks flushing and her eyes lighting up. "I bet Clarissa Hanover's spirit is keeping watch over the Bluff, pushing people off, just like the legend says."

"I have to admit, Amanda, I didn't believe this whole thing at first, not really. But I'm starting to," Keera said with a slight shudder.

"It's creepy, isn't it?" Amanda agreed. "I guess this means we'll have to write in a bigger part for Missy. It *is* a fitting part for her, don't you think?" Amanda added with a wan smile.

Keera nodded in agreement. Then the two girls put their heads together to finish writing the script.

After several hours of rehashing the dialogue and the staging, Amanda announced wearily, "I think we're done, don't you?"

Keera looked blurrily down at the last words scribbled on the page. "Yes," she said. "It's so chilling, I don't think we'll even need the real screams and sobs."

"Well, we'll hear them anyway," Amanda promised.

Keera stretched, covering her mouth with her hand to hide a sleepy yawn.

"I guess I better get going," Amanda said, reluctant to leave Keera's warm and cheery room to return to her own cream-colored palace in Cliffside Heights.

"Wait, Amanda. I almost forgot . . ." Keera said, jolting herself awake.

"Forgot what?"

"Well, it's about rehearsal on Friday night. Jamar's doing his gig at the Torch Club that night—"

"You mean he can't come to rehearsal?" Amanda asked in dismay.

"No—I mean, yes, he'll be there. But I want to go hear him play after that, and I was wondering if you'd like to go, too. I was going to ask Hero, but . . ."

"I'd love to go. And you can ask Hero about it separately, I guess. I mean, obviously, we're not going to come together, but I'll be there, so long as I don't actually get killed during rehearsal!" Amanda joked.

"Great," Keera said, relieved. "I'm glad you're coming. I really wanted to go, for Jamar's sake, but I didn't feel comfortable going to the Torch Club all by myself."

"Won't Jamar be with you?" Amanda asked.

"You know how he is. He's going to dash off after rehearsal in his own car to get there to help set up, and then he'll be playing all night, lost in the music. He won't be likely to pay much attention to me, but he needs to know that I'm there," Keera explained with a sigh.

Amanda arched her eyebrow and gave Keera a questioning glance. "Is something wrong?" she asked. "I've been so busy feeling sorry for myself, I haven't even had a chance to find out how things are going with you two."

"No, nothing's wrong," Keera said slowly.

Amanda pounced on the bed beside Keera. "I know that look, Keera Johnson. Come on. I bared my heart and soul to you. Tell me," Amanda demanded.

"It's nothing." Keera paused. "It's just, there's this new guy . . ."

"Aha. I thought so," Amanda cried. "Tell me more!"

"There's nothing to tell, Amanda, really. Jordan Harris has been talking to me a lot lately, just to be friendly."

"Jordan Harris!" Amanda squealed in delight. "That cute senior who's going to be the pick of every basket-ball-playing college in the country? How cool! Keera, you sly thing!"

Keera blushed right down to the roots of her hair.

"Has he kissed you yet?" Amanda asked.

"Amanda!" Keera said, shocked.

"Come on, Keera. You can't tell me you haven't thought about it, at least. Jordan's practically the cutest guy in all of Cliffside County."

"Well . . . I think he's come awfully close," Keera said in a low voice.

"I knew it!" Amanda said. "How could you start liking Jordan Harris and not mention it to me? I can't believe it. What are you going to say to Jamar?"

"Nothing," Keera said firmly. "I

didn't say I liked Jordan Harris. I mean, Jordan hasn't actually ever asked me out. Every time it seems as though he's about to, something happens to interrupt him—like Jamar showing up."

"So Jamar knows about Jordan and that's why he wants you to go to the gig on Friday night?" Amanda asked.

"No. Definitely not. Jamar doesn't know anything at all. I mean, there isn't anything to know," Keera reiterated. "Jamar jokes about me liking Jordan Harris, but he doesn't have a clue that I really do."

"So, you *do* like Jordan Harris!" Amanda said triumphantly.

Keera hung her head in defeat. "Well, I think I do."

"And you wouldn't exactly turn him down if he asked you out, right?" Amanda badgered her.

"Okay, I give up. No, I wouldn't turn him down if he asked." Keera laughed in mock surrender.

"So is the concert at the Torch Club going to be the kiss-off for Jamar?" Amanda asked.

Keera shrugged. "I don't know,

Amanda. I really don't know how I feel anymore. I mean, I still love Jamar, the way he makes me laugh, the way he looks at me, and touches me, and stuff, but . . ."

"But . . . " Amanda echoed Keera.

"But it's Jordan's face that I keep seeing in my dreams. Sometimes he seems so real, so close, that I feel like I could almost reach out and touch his strong, muscled back or feel his fingers stroking my face," Keera said softly. "I feel like I could lose myself entirely if I kissed him."

"Wow, you've got it bad for him, don't you?"

Keera lowered her eyes and nodded her head.

"So, why go to the Torch Club with Jamar and prolong the agony?" Amanda wanted to know.

"Because I think I owe him that," Keera said. "After all, it's Jamar's big night. I want to be there to share it with him, even if we don't stay together."

"I really admire you, Keera," Amanda said. "I'm not sure I could do that for Hero, if I was thinking about some other guy the way that you're thinking about Jordan."

"Well, it's not like anything's actually happening," Keera said. "It's all just in my dreams at the moment."

"Yeah, but dreams sometimes have a funny way of coming true."

Amanda glanced over at the clock-radio on Keera's dresser.

"Ohmigosh, it's eleven-thirty, and I told the ice queen I'd be home by eleven. I'm going to get grounded for sure if I don't split," Amanda said, gathering up the pages she and Keera had worked on that evening.

"Okay, I'll see you at the station tomorrow," Keera promised.

At the door, Keera gave Amanda a quick hug. "See you tomorrow, girl-friend," Keera said warmly.

"Thanks for listening, Keera," Amanda said over her shoulder as she headed for her car.

"And you," Keera acknowledged. She waited until Amanda had driven away before closing the front door.

As she rested her cheek on the door-jamb, Keera thought again about how it would feel to have Jordan Harris holding her right at that moment, tilting her head back and pressing his lips to hers, kissing her until she couldn't even breathe.

"Girl, what are you doing?" Mrs. Johnson called from the top of the stairway.

"Nothing, Ma. Just getting ready to go to bed," Keera answered, embarrassed.

"Well, get going, then," Mrs. Johnson admonished her, turning on her heel and heading for her own bedroom. "It's bad enough you're yakking and talking instead of studying. Now you're kissing doorways. Fool girl worrying about fool boys. Where did I go wrong?" Mrs. Johnson mumbled to herself.

Slowly, Keera headed upstairs. But she wasn't listening to a word her mother was saying. Keera's only thoughts were of Jordan, and what it would be like when her dreams finally came true.

# Chapter Eleven

*T*he next day, as Keera was walking away from school on her way to the KSS station to go over the script, she heard footsteps running behind her.

"Keera! Hey, Keera, wait up," Jordan called.

Yes! Keera said quietly to herself. She'd been hoping all day that Jordan would come over to her.

"What's your hurry, girlfriend?" Jordan asked, falling easily into step beside her.

"We're having our first rehearsal for the KSS Halloween show, and I guess I'm a little excited about it," Keera said.

"Let my wheels be your chariot," Jordan said with a gracious sweep of his hand.

Keera tilted her head and smiled at

Jordan. "No, I think I'd rather walk today, if you don't mind," she answered.

"Mind if I walk with you?" Jordan asked.

"I was hoping you'd ask."

"You were?" Jordan seemed surprised.

"Uh-huh," Keera said with an impish grin in Jordan's direction.

Jordan and Keera walked along in silence for a while, the only sound the leaves crackling under their feet. Finally, Jordan spoke.

"Uh, Keera," he began, kicking a rock as they walked, "I have something I've been wanting to ask you." He paused.

"Yes?" Keera replied. Her heart was thumping so loudly in her ears, she was sure Jordan could hear it.

"Well, it's kind of hard to ask you," Jordan said.

I can't believe Jordan Harris, basketball superstar, cutest guy in the world, is so shy that he's having trouble asking someone like me out, Keera thought in amazement. Up to now he had seemed so smooth!

"What I mean to say is, we're friends, now, aren't we?" Jordan asked. "I consider you my good friend, and I hope that you consider me yours."

"Of course I do, Jordan," Keera replied softly. She stopped walking, to make it easier for him to speak to her.

Jordan put both his hands on Keera's shoulders, gazing deeply into her sea-green eyes.

Keera held her breath. The blood was pounding in her head. She could hardly wait for the moment when Jordan would bend his head close, then ever-so-gently touch his lips to hers. Then, in one passionate move, he would pull her close to his hard body, crush her with his muscular arms, and kiss her so deeply she would faint.

"Keera, I really need you to tutor me in chemistry, or my basketball career is ruined," Jordan said. "Do you think you can? Please say yes."

Keera blinked as though waking from a dream. With a small movement, she shrugged out from under Jordan's grasp.

"Jordan, did you just say that you want me . . . to . . . tutor you in chemistry?" Keera asked slowly, as if translating something into English. Her voice rose shrilly at the end of the question.

Jordan nodded. "Yes. I've been wanting to ask you for the past month, but I didn't have the nerve. I'm not used to asking for help, and you're only a junior. I was afraid you'd laugh at me. But now I feel like I know you well enough to ask. I'll never be recruited to any of the Division One NCAA schools unless I can pass chemistry this semester," Jordan explained.

Keera didn't know whether she wanted to cry or laugh. Suddenly, it was as though she were seeing this scene from outside herself. She watched Jordan babble on about his chemistry grades and how much her tutoring would mean to him, until Keera felt she was a million miles away.

Finally, she realized there was only way to get rid of Jordan so she could mull over this humiliation on her own.

"Yes, Jordan. I'd be happy to tutor you in chemistry," Keera said quietly.

"You would? That's great," Jordan said. He grabbed Keera and gave her a huge hug.

How ironic, Keera thought. This is just what I've been dreaming about, and now it doesn't matter at all.

Stepping back, out of the hug, Keera said, "Listen, Jordan, I've really got to hustle, or I'm going to be late."

"Sure, anything you say," Jordan said.

"Catch up with me tomorrow, and we'll figure out a good time, okay?" Keera called behind her as she broke into a trot toward the KSS station. Jordan is a jerk, Jordan is a jerk, Keera kept saying to herself. She figuring if she said it enough times, by the time she got to the KSS station, she might actually believe it.

Neither Jordan nor Keera noticed Jamar trailing them along the bike path. Jamar had been wondering who the couple was standing on the sidewalk up ahead. Then he realized the girl in that couple was Keera!

Pedaling furiously, Jamar caught up

to them in time to see Jordan hug Keera and hear Keera calling back to Jordan.

Jamar braked to a sudden halt, not wanting either of them to notice him. I can't believe this, he said to himself. He didn't know what to do next. How could he ride on to meet Keera at the station, knowing she was two-timing him with Jordan Harris? And how was he going to get through the next few days, the gig, the Halloween Dance, the Halloween show? Was he just supposed to pretend everything was normal?

Jamar stood there for a very long time, not knowing what to feel or where to go.

Finally, he began to pedal slowly toward the KSS station. I'll just have to play it by ear, he decided to himself. I'll see what Keera's like, and I'll take it from there.

Maybe his best friend, Rogue Jelsen, had been right after all. Perhaps brainy chicks like Keera couldn't possibly care about someone like him for long. But Jordan Harris was no rocket scientist either. The thought only made him feel worse.

Glancing at his watch, Jamar realized he was going to be seriously late unless he got going. Deciding to put his unhappiness on hold, Jamar shoved on his headphones and pumped up the volume, pedaling as fast as he could.

By the time Jamar got to the station, everyone—Drew, Keera, Amanda, Tyler, Hero, and Missy—was waiting for him. "Hey, all. Sorry I'm late," Jamar said. He noted Tyler's presence with surprise.

"Tyler, what are you doing, checking on your daddy's investments?" Jamar joked.

"Amanda asked me to come and watch the drama," Tyler said, lounging back in his chair. "It's been pretty interesting so far, and we haven't even started yet," he added with a sly glance at Missy, who gave him a secret smile.

"Okay, now that you're all here, let's see what you've got," Drew said, eager to hear the final script.

Amanda handed Jamar his copy of the script.

"You can use this to finalize the score you've been working on. Keera and I stayed pretty close to the outline, with a few significant changes," Amanda told him.

"How is your score coming?" Keera asked. "I forgot to ask, we've all been so busy lately."

"You especially," Jamar said pointedly to Keera. "It's cool," he added nonchalantly. "I'm almost done. I've just been waiting for you girls to figure out the grand finale."

"Okay, here's the plan," Amanda said. "We'll work out the staging when we rehearse at the Bluff. Right now we'll just read through the script."

"Sounds good," Drew said.

"Keera's going to start by telling about the various versions of the legend we've all heard and give some of the background info on spooky, unexplainable things that have happened on the Bluff. There was a girl in 1927 who claimed someone was trying to push her over the edge, only no one else was on the Bluff; in 1934 a man threw himself over the side on Halloween night, because he heard the screams and couldn't bear the sound; a reporter in 1987 ended up 'on the rocks' when she was researching the Bluff legend."

"Did that really happen?" Missy asked skeptically.

"According to the articles in the *Cliffside Daily*, it did," Amanda retorted. "Then, we'll segue into the 'real' story behind the legend. We'll act out what *really* happened that night, according to the newspaper articles."

"So, let's get started," Hero said impatiently.

"Fine. Let's get started," Amanda snapped back at him.

Keera began to read the introductory narrative in a low, hushed voice. As the drama proceeded, tension crackled in the room.

The scenes between Amanda and Hero, as Mariah and Winston, made each of them noticeably uncomfortable. When Mariah had to say, "I've loved you with all of my heart,"

Amanda's face paled.

When Winston had to say, "And I vow to love you for all of eternity and beyond," Hero choked.

Missy, as Clarissa, was frighteningly evil. She wormed her way into Winston Hanover's confidence as easily as she had won over Hero. She plotted her revenge against Mariah and Winston, using Jess Wiley as her unwitting tool. It was hard to know where Amanda and Keera's writing stopped and Missy's acting began.

By the end of the reading, even Drew expected to hear screams and sobs in the wind. Solemnly, he applauded their effort. "That was some piece of writing, Amanda and Keera."

Amanda gave Drew an appreciative smile. Then she glanced over at Hero, who was gazing at Amanda with a mixture of emotions whirling behind his eyes. For a moment, Amanda's heart leaped, thinking maybe . . .

Then Missy possessively laid her hand on Hero's arm. Amanda flinched.

"Good acting, all of you, although Amanda and Hero could use a little extra practice," Drew went on. "That was an outstanding performance you gave, Missy."

Missy flashed Drew a brilliant smile. "Thank you," she purred.

"I think Scott Enterprises will be satisfied with the end result," Drew added.

"Oh, did Scott Enterprises have something to do with this production?" Tyler asked in feigned surprise.

"They're the ones who suggested you do a scary Halloween special to begin with, right?" Missy said helpfully.

"How did you know that?" Amanda asked sharply.

Tyler threw Missy a deadly glance. Flustered, she tried to recover quickly. "Oh, I don't know. I guess my Hero must have told me that." Missy squeezed Hero's arm.

"Anyway, crew, I think you've done a fine job. Jamar, when can we have the music?" Drew asked.

"I'll copy the tape and leave it in the music room. JellyJam's meeting here tonight to record the finale, if anyone wants to stay and hear it," Jamar said with a glance at Keera.

"I'd like to," Keera responded.

Jamar looked over at her and shrugged. "That's cool," he said unenthusiastically.

What's with him? Keera wondered. He's acting like he could care less about me, and that's not like Jamar. When he headed into the music room, Keera followed.

"Hero, take me home now," Missy commanded.

Just as Hero was about to reluctantly oblige, Drew called to him from his office. "Hero, I'd like to go over some details on the equipment and props for the show with you."

Looking almost relieved, Hero said, "Sorry, Missy. I've got to talk to Drew, unless you want to wait around . . ."

"Never mind," Missy answered shortly. She threw a sinister glance at Amanda, who was trying to hide her delight that Hero was letting Missy go home by herself by pretending to go through the papers and messages piled on her desk.

"Well, call me later, Hero," Missy said petulantly, unhappy about leaving Hero and Amanda together.

"Right," Hero said. "Later, Missy." He retreated quickly into Drew's office.

"See you on the Bluff, Mandy," Missy added with a menacing softness.

"Right," Amanda said, echoing Hero's tone.

"Let's split and go for a ride," Tyler said to Amanda.

Glancing toward Drew's office, Amanda said, "Uh, I think I'll stay here. I have to talk to Drew about something, and I don't want to interrupt him and Hero."

"Okay," Tyler said. "I'll take a walk and be back to pick you up in about an hour?" he asked.

"Sure, Tyler. Don't rush, though."

Tyler left the station and looked up and down the street, hoping to catch up with Missy. Spotting her about two-thirds of a block away, Tyler easily overtook her. They walked toward Cliffside Heights together.

"What do you want, Tyler?" Missy asked, looking around anxiously.

"We're not supposed to be seen together in public, remember?"

"I know, but everyone who might notice is at the KSS station, and I had to talk to you. My parents cut off my private phone when my father found out I'd plugged back into Scott Enterprises and started giving out fake orders."

Tyler laughed scornfully. "Can you believe that guy Drew, thinking Scott Enterprises cares what kind of show KSS-TV does?" Abruptly, he grew serious. "You seem to be right where you want to be with Hero," he said, a tinge of jealousy in his voice.

"Yes, you could say that," Missy said smugly. Then she looked over and caught Tyler's expression. "Don't tell me you're seriously jealous of me with Hero?"

"No, not at all. Besides, my end isn't so bad. Snuggling up to Amanda isn't as tough as it looks, even if it is just to get back at her for humiliating me last summer," Tyler said. "Now, back to business. Hero is taking you to the dance on Halloween night, isn't he?"

Missy hesitated for a moment.

"Come on, Missy, you've got to be kidding. With you all over him all the time, he hasn't asked you to the dance? Is the guy crazy? After all, you are Homecoming Queen," Tyler said in exasperation.

"Look, Tyler, it's not a problem," Missy said with a confidence she didn't entirely feel. "I mean, it's not like he's going with anyone else. Even if we don't arrive together, I'll still be on him like a second skin. Besides, we're in the show together, so he'll have to stick close to me. Don't give it a second thought. You'll have plenty of opportunities to do what you need to do. Besides, we'll be able to set most of it up tomorrow night after the rehearsal. So, you take care of Mandy and let me worry about Hero."

"With pleasure," Tyler said. Suddenly, with cat-like quickness, Tyler grabbed Missy, pulled her to him, and kissed her hard on the mouth.

"Tyler, cut it out. We'll have plenty of time for that later," Missy warned, pulling away and checking around to see if anyone had seen them together.

At the entrance to Cliffside Heights, Missy slipped in through the gate, leaving Tyler behind in the quickening darkness. Watching her, Tyler smiled happily to himself.

Ah, revenge—it's a tough job, but somebody's got to do it, Tyler thought with a grin, as he turned back toward the station to retrieve Amanda.

Tyler and Missy didn't know it, but Samantha Walker, Amanda's used-to-be best friend had been walking behind them. Samantha, Tyler, and Amanda had all been friends once. But after this summer, when Tyler had used Samantha in an attempt to win back Amanda, Samantha had steered clear of them both.

Samantha had finally realized what a creep Tyler was. She sorely missed her friendship with Amanda, but Amanda wasn't having anything to do with her. "I don't trust you anymore, Samantha," was the last thing Amanda had said to her when she'd hung up the phone after Samantha's latest apologetic call.

Although Samantha had been

hanging out with a different crowd this fall, she couldn't help but notice how Missy Hanover had been all over Hero. So she was very surprised to see Tyler and Missy that Thursday afternoon, walking home together and looking for all the world like they were a tight couple.

Slipping into the cover of the wooded area that ran along the sidewalk, Samantha managed to get close enough to hear Missy say, "You take care of Mandy and let me worry about Hero." She stared in disbelief as Tyler grabbed Missy and kissed her.

"Ohmigosh, Tyler's got another plot in the works, and Missy Hanover is part of it," Samantha whispered incredulously to herself. "I've got to tell Amanda."

Samantha waited just long enough for Missy and Tyler to disappear before she sprinted home. But just as she was about to dial Amanda's number, Samantha replaced the phone in its cradle.

Amanda would never believe her, not without proof. She would have to get something more on them, something Amanda would really believe. Samantha thought for a moment. Her gaze rested on the new camera with a zoom lens that her parents had given her for her birthday.

Samantha smiled as a plan of her own began to take shape.

# Chapter Twelve

*B*ack at the KSS station, Drew had finished going over the props and had worked out some basic stage directions for Hero to incorporate into the rehearsal at the Bluff. Drew and Hero agreed to go over to the Bluff tomorrow afternoon, after school, to set up everything for that night's rehearsal.

Amanda had been fussing around her desk, pushing papers around, sharpening pencils, doing anything to keep busy, in the hope of getting a chance to speak with Hero before Tyler returned.

Since they had broken up, Amanda hadn't had a single opportunity to speak to Hero. But today, during the reading, Amanda had felt something stir in her heart when she told Hero, as Winston, how much she loved him.

And she'd seen a flicker in Hero's eyes that made her think he still loved her, too. Amanda had to know how Hero really felt about her.

Pretending to be unaware of Amanda's presence, Hero stood in Drew's doorway, talking and joking until Amanda was about to scream from frustration. Finally, Hero turned and walked into the main office, glancing at Amanda as he went over to his desk.

"That was a pretty good piece of writing you and Keera did," Hero told her.

"Thanks. What happened to your hand?" Amanda asked, looking with concern at the large bandage wrapped around Hero's knuckles.

"It's nothing, I just banged it," Hero said. "So . . . how are you these days?"

Amanda's heart began race. He still cared!

"I'm . . . okay," Amanda said, her voice trembling a bit. "And you?"

"Oh, fine, you know," Hero said, pushing back that persistent lock of hair that always fell across his forehead.

"Are you taking Missy to the dance on Saturday?" Amanda asked.

"Are you going to the dance with Tyler?" Hero asked in return.

Just then Tyler entered the room, in time to hear Hero's last question.

"Of course, she's going to the dance with me. I wouldn't have it any other way," Tyler said, smoothly placing his arms around Amanda's shoulders.

Immediately, Hero's eyes turned to stone. "See you there, then," he said carelessly, giving Amanda a cold, level stare.

"Hero, I—" Amanda started to say.

"I've got to talk to Jamar about something," Hero interrupted her. "Later," he added, then turned on his heel and went down the corridor to the music room.

"Are you ready, Amanda?" Tyler asked impatiently. "How about that ride now?"

"I'm really kind of tired, Tyler. Would you mind just taking me home?" Amanda asked.

"Sure, if that's what you want," Tyler said, ushering Amanda out the door.

Just as Hero was about to enter the music room, Keera stalked out in such a hurry that she almost knocked him down.

"Hey, what's your rush, girl?" Hero asked with surprise.

"No rush. Just making room for Jamar's ego," Keera snapped. She gave Jamar a last angry look before taking off down the corridor. Moments later, the station door slammed so hard that the glass in the studio shook.

"Man, she sure is mad about something. What did you say to her?" Hero asked.

"It's not what I said, dude. It's what I wouldn't say," Jamar told him.

"Sounds heavy. What's up?" Hero asked.

"I've got the senior blues," Jamar said, playing a blues sequence on the keyboard.

Hero smiled. "I know what you mean," he told Jamar. "But I thought things between you and Keera were cool."

"So did I," Jamar said. "Until today." He added a crash of discordant chords to emphasize his discontent.

"Cough it up, man. What's going on with you and Keera?"

"Oh, nothing much. My heart's lying broken all over the road between here and school, 'cause that's where I saw Keera and Jordan Harris hugging and arranging to meet."

"Come on, man. Get real. What's happening?" Hero said, not believing a word Jamar had said.

"I'm telling you the truth, dude. That's what's happening, believe it or not."

Hero stared at Jamar. "Jordan Harris, huh. I wouldn't have thought he was Keera's type."

"Thanks, man. But, as my friend Rogue always told me, I'm not exactly her type, either. Not to mention that I'm not a senior and might never be one. I don't have the muscles, the good looks, the fancy car, or a letter sweater going for me," Jamar said unhappily, ticking off his faults as he picked at the keys on the keyboard.

Hero thought for a minute. "You know, this just doesn't feel right to me.

I mean, it's not like I keep track of stuff like this, but Missy mentioned that Jordan Harris was going out with Maya Turner, the head cheerleader. They're planning a dual costume for the Halloween dance," he said.

A small bud of hope began to blossom in Jamar's heart. "Really?" he asked.

"Pretty sure," Hero told him. He slapped Jamar on the back. "Cheer up, guy. That girl is yours. Any girl who'd leave a room as angry as Keera just did has to care. And that makes you a luckier dude than I am," Hero added, playing a forlorn couple of notes on the keyboard himself.

"Aw, come on, Hero. Do you think I'm a fool? You go from Amanda Townsend to Missy Hanover in one week, and I'm supposed to feel sorry for you?" Jamar teased him.

"Yeah, well, Missy's convenient, that's about all," Hero said.

"Convenient? Like how?" Jamar asked.

"You know, she's a warm body. Somebody to take away the pain of seeing Amanda running around arm in arm with the almighty Tyler Scott," Hero complained.

"Well, if you've got to have a warm body, Missy's about as warm as you can get," Jamar commented with a gleam in his eye.

"Yeah," Hero replied with a sheepish grin. "Too bad I'm not interested. I just can't stop thinking about Amanda. It kills me to see her with Tyler all the time. But there's no breaking through, 'cause Tyler's always around," Hero complained.

"Try calling her at home," Jamar suggested.

"No kidding. Don't you think I've tried? But the ice queen, Mrs. Townsend, always answers and says Amanda's not home. And I know she's not giving her the messages. It's not like Amanda's mother is sorry we're broken up," Hero added bitterly.

"So what are you going to do?" Jamar asked.

"I don't know," Hero replied. "I keep hoping I'll wake up one morning, and it will all be right again. But with Tyler around, that doesn't seem likely. Anyway, I'm outta here. Want to grab some dinner?"

"Sorry, dude, no can do. The boys in the band are due here soon, and I've got to finish my tune," Jamar told him, beginning to refocus on the notes he'd been writing before Hero walked in.

"No problem. See you mañana, at the Bluff," Hero said, slapping Jamar five before exiting the room.

Hero listened to his own steps echoing emptily through the corridor. He felt like talking to someone, but there was no one to talk to. For a brief moment, he thought about going over to Missy's house. But the moment passed. What he really wanted to do was throw himself at the foot of Amanda's couch and have her run her hands through his hair, her cool fingers stroking his temples. He longed to pull her beautiful face down to his so he could consume her lips.

Oh, Amanda, Hero groaned to himself, wishing with all his heart that he had the right to just drive up to her house and go in.

But remembering how Tyler possessively draped his arm around Amanda's shoulder made Hero stiffen in anger. He knew this whole mess was Tyler's doing. But at the moment there wasn't anything Hero could do about it.

Swiftly Hero pulled on his helmet, hurried out to his motorcycle, and roared off, spinning almost out of control into the night.

# Chapter Thirteen

*T*he next day at four o'clock, Amanda stood proudly in the doorway of the gym. The special effects of the strobe lighting, the cobwebs festooned from the ceiling, the pop-up skeletons in the corners, and the spooky laughter emanating from hidden speakers had turned the gym into the perfect nightmare.

The rest of the volunteers were going to set up the booths tomorrow afternoon, so Amanda could finally turn her attention back to the KSS Halloween special and that night's rehearsal.

Without looking where she was going, Amanda stepped back to admire the ceiling decorations. "Hey, watch out," a voice called from behind her. A pair of strong, muscular arms grabbed her around the waist.

Frightened, Amanda turned around and found herself face to face with Tyler.

"Oh, Tyler, you scared me," Amanda said, heaving a sigh of relief. "The gym looks so spooky that I'm a little jumpy."

Slipping his arm around Amanda's shoulders and pulling her toward him, Tyler murmured into Amanda's hair, "I can think of something we can do to make you less tense."

"Tyler!" Amanda said indignantly.

"Sorry, Amanda. I guess Halloween is getting to me, too. Come on, let's go for a ride before the rehearsal starts. Just you and me, under the stars."

Amanda moved uncomfortably in the circle of Tyler's arms. This past week, spent with Tyler instead of Hero, had seemed almost surreal to Amanda. And everywhere she looked, she saw Hero and Missy: Missy hanging on Hero, Hero laughing with Missy. It was almost too much to bear.

"Hey, Amanda. There's a call for you in the main office. Something about a shuttle bus to the Bluff?" someone shouted down the hall.

"Oh, great," Amanda said. Shrugging out of Tyler's grasp, Amanda raced down the hall. "I'll be at rehearsal and then out for the night, so I'll see you tomorrow," Amanda called, grateful for a simple way to escape from Tyler. He really was hard to shake. Amanda felt light as a bird without the weight of Tyler's arm around her shoulders.

At seven o'clock sharp, Hero roared up on his motorcycle, spraying gravel and dirt on the white Mustang convertible already parked at the Bluff. Pulling off his helmet, Hero looked around for Amanda. In the early darkness and misty fog that hung over the Bluff, it was hard to tell whether anyone was standing near the edge of the cliff.

Hero fumbled around in the dark for the switch to the floodlights that he and Drew had set up that afternoon. Suddenly, there was a strange sound behind him.

"Ooooooooooooh."

Hero whirled around, startled. Then

he saw Amanda's laughing face.

"Gotcha," Amanda said, tapping Hero lightly on the shoulder and running away before he could tag her back.

"Oh, yeah?" Hero growled. Switching on the floodlights, so the Bluff was bathed in light, Hero chased after her. When they came to the edge of the cliff, he grabbed her, holding her over the fifty-foot drop to the rocks and water below.

"Uh-oh. Good thing it's not Halloween night. Otherwise we might both end up over the edge, like those people you and Keera wrote about," Hero teased.

Amanda gasped and pulled herself free.

"That's not funny, Hero. Those so-called accidents really did happen." Then, with a mischievous grin, she added, "You didn't look too sure of yourself in the dark, when I crept up on you just two minutes ago."

For a moment, Hero forgot that he and Amanda had broken up. He wanted to crush her to him, feel her lips clinging to his. Amanda looked so pale and fragile, his arms ached to hold her.

"Hey, you two. Practicing your parts already?" a cheerful voice rang out. Missy Hanover walked rapidly over to where Hero and Amanda stood.

Amanda quickly withdrew out of the light and walked back over to the cliff's edge. With a jolt, Hero remembered that Amanda wasn't his any longer.

"Where's your car?" Hero asked, realizing he hadn't heard Missy drive up to the Bluff.

"Oh, I left it at the bottom of the Bluff road. I don't like taking it up on the gravel, and I thought I'd walk up here by myself and surprise you." Missy moved close to him, reaching up to kiss him lightly.

Hero drew back, remembering that Amanda was standing in the shadows. But Missy pulled Hero's head down, kissing him hungrily.

They were suddenly interrupted by the tooting of a car horn.

"Yo, Hero. Missy. Do your kissing

elsewhere. This is the killing place, not the parking place," Jamar teased, jumping out of the battered old Jeep he'd borrowed from Rogue.

Keera stepped out of the other side of the Jeep. "Where's Amanda?" she asked.

Hero looked around, squinting against the floodlights. "She's roaming around somewhere by herself."

"Brave girl," Keera commented with a slight shudder.

"There's nothing to worry about—it's not Halloween night," Hero remarked with a wink to Jamar.

"Right," Jamar answered with a grin.

"Stop it, you guys. Don't you make fun of poor Mandy. If she wants to believe in this whole legend thing, then you just go ahead and let her. Why, I believed in fairy tales for the longest time when I was a kid," Missy offered, her voice dripping with insincerity.

Amanda, who upon spotting Keera and Jamar's arrival, had started walking back toward the center of the Bluff, overheard Missy's words.

"Thanks a lot, Missy," Amanda said, stepping out of the darkness. "It means a lot to me to know that you really know how I feel."

"Okay, girls. Truce," Hero said. "Let's run through the show. The faster we do it, the faster we can get out of here and go someplace warmer."

"True enough—and I've got to be at the Torch Club at nine sharp to get ready for our set," Jamar said, impatiently dancing around.

"Okay, let's get into position," Hero directed, looking at the script. He quickly told everybody where to stand and when they should move.

"Be sure to creep in front of the camera so we see you sneaking up into the bushes," he told Jamar, who was playing Jess. "Then the camera in the bushes will take over, and the TV viewers will see what happens next as if they were standing with you at the scene," Hero finished explaining.

"That's a really brilliant piece of direction, Hero," Amanda said, impressed by how much thought Hero had put into the staging.

145

"Thanks," Hero said modestly, giving Amanda a small smile.

"Let's roll," Jamar urged them.

"Okay, now!" Hero said, turning on the camera and beginning to film.

"Action!" Keera called.

Keera began her narrative, walking toward the cliff as she spoke. She ended her introduction by saying, "And now, here is the real story of what happened on Cliffside Bluff on that fateful Halloween night of 1894."

CLARISSA: But Winston, I am so much prettier and wealthier than Mariah Wiley. Why won't you even consider me?

WINSTON: Don't be ridiculous, little girl. What do you know about such things? And what does Mariah Wiley have to do with this? What is Mariah to me?

CLARISSA: Oh, Winston. Men can be such fools sometimes. I know everything you do, everything about you. I love you, Winston—don't you know that?

WINSTON: Such foolish talk, Clarissa. You are just a mere slip of a girl. You talk of love, but what do you know of it? Of course, you love me, as a brother, as a cousin. And I love you, in that same way. But we were not meant for each other, my darling girl. Hold your love true for another, as I do mine.

CLARISSA: I know enough to understand deceit and deception when I see them.

WINSTON: What do you mean?

CLARISSA: I know that you think you will be eloping with Mariah tonight.

WINSTON: What? How the devil—

CLARISSA: I told you, I know things. I listen. I see. I am not such an inconsequential child as you might think.

WINSTON: You must tell no one. I warn you.

CLARISSA: Oh, Winston, I would never tell. But don't you

see, you will be hurt. How do I know of your elopement? From Mariah, who else? And I also know that Mariah will not be marrying you tonight, or any other night. I tell you, Mariah is in love with Jess, her own cousin. She intends to tell you that this very night. Why, Jess intends to tell you himself and put an end to you and Mariah.

WINSTON: How, pray tell, do you come to know that?

CLARISSA: I told you, I know things—and you'd be well advised to listen to my counsel.

WINSTON: Away with you, girl. And tell no one what we've discussed here.

CLARISSA: As you wish, my love. But you will see.


In a hushed voice, Keera, spoke up again. "Later that evening, while all the town was having a riotous celebration at the Halloween Costume Ball, a girlish figure slipped away from the crowd and whispered to a young man."

CLARISSA: It's all set. Mariah wants you to meet her at the Bluff at midnight. She intends to tell Winston then that she will marry only you and not him.

JESS: Are you sure, Clarissa? I don't understand why Mariah speaks only through you and not to me directly.

CLARISSA: She fears Winston's temper—for your sake. Mariah would not have him angered in public, for who knows what might happen? And she trusts me, because I have been her friend—and because she knows Winston adores me. I am his most beloved cousin, you know. He would do anything in the world for me, as would I do for him.

JESS: I'm not afraid of Winston. His temper means nothing to me. I am much stronger than he is, and so is my love for Mariah.

CLARISSA: Yes, Mariah knows that, and she loves you for your strength. She is hoping you will carry her off in your arms tonight, and she will never have to look at Winston again. Hurry, they must already be on their separate ways to the Bluff. Take care—Winston's temper is fierce.

Again, Keera spoke up. "Soon it was almost midnight. Two figures roamed the opposite ends of the Bluff, searching for each other. The moon, which had shone so brightly just moments earlier, passed behind a thick cloud, and the Bluff fell into total darkness.

"Undetected, a third figure crept into the bushes across from the cliff's edge and remained to watch the unfolding events . . . while a fourth lumbered up the gravel road with a dark purpose in mind . . ."

MARIAH: My love. Where are you?

WINSTON: Mariah? I'm here by the cliff. Where have you been?

MARIAH: Searching for you. This has been a most terrible night—I have been frightened almost out of my wits. Someone sent me a letter warning me not to marry you. It said only harm could come to us both.

WINSTON: Nonsense. There is no one who knows of our plans.

MARIAH: My darling, there is something I must tell you now.

WINSTON: Say it then. Say it quickly and then let us be gone.

MARIAH: I've loved you with all of my heart, and I always will—from the first moment I saw you until the day I die.

WINSTON: And I vow to love you for all eternity and beyond.

JESS: Let go of her!

WINSTON: Who speaks so? Who are you?

JESS: I said, let go of her. She doesn't love you. Mariah, darling, you are mine at last. Unhand her, and leave her unharmed.

WINSTON: Never.

JESS: I said, let her go!

MARIAH: Winston. My love. Oh, Wiiiiiiiiinnnnnnnnnnnnston.

WINSTON: Mariaaaaaaaaaaaaaaahh!

JESS: Mariaaaaaaaaaaaaaaaaaah! You killed her, you swine. You killed her. And now I'll kill you!!!

WINSTON: Mariaaaaaaaaaaaaaaah.

JESS: (Sobbing)

In the silence that followed, Keera spoke again.

"When the town marshal came to take Jess Wiley away, all Jess could do was sob Mariah's name. No one was sure what had happened that night on the Bluff. The only thing anyone knew was that Mariah Wiley and Winston Hanover were dead, their bodies battered and smashed at the base of the cliff.

"It wasn't until several days later that

an eyewitness came forward. It was Clarissa Hanover. The fourteen-year-old never explained what she was doing there that night. But she told the jury how Jess tried to wrest Mariah from Winston's grasp and ended up killing her, then turned his fury on Winston as well. Based on her testimony, Jess was hanged in the town square on Thanksgiving Day, and no further thought was given to the matter.

"Clarissa, deeply affected by the incident, was never the same. She roamed the Bluff aimlessly for the next several years. And in her twenty-first year, on Halloween night, seven years to the day that Winston and Mariah had been killed, she flung herself off the cliff, calling Winston's name as she went.

"And so, as the midnight hour approaches, we at KSS await the screams of legend, the souls of Mariah, Winston, Jess—and perhaps even Clarissa—who haunt this Bluff on Allhallows Eve."

"Cut!" Hero shouted. "That was pretty good, folks," he said, running over to the camera to shut off the tape.

"If something happens tomorrow and we can't do it live, we can air the tape and cut back to the live action for the screams."

"Cool, dude. Now I've got to split. See you girls there," Jamar said to Amanda and Keera, running off without so much as a kiss for Keera.

"I thought that went pretty well," Amanda said, "although I'm feeling a little spooked up here now. I feel like someone really *is* watching us."

"Sure, Mandy. It's Clarissa's spirit. I felt it myself when I was hiding in the bushes," Missy teased as Hero came up beside her.

"Right," Amanda said evenly. Then she turned away from Missy and Hero. "Come on, Keera. Let's go."

"Okay with me," Keera said. She felt somewhat chilled herself, but she wasn't sure whether it was from the cool night air or Jamar's cold shoulder.

"Where are you two off to in such a hurry?" Hero asked.

"We're supposed to be checking out Jamar's band at the Torch Club. Want to come?" Keera asked. She bit her lip as soon as the words left her mouth. She kept forgetting Amanda and Hero had broken up.

Hero glanced at Amanda, whose eyes were shining at the possibility.

Possessively, Missy coiled her arm around Hero's and looked directly into his eyes. "How about we leave the floodlights on and go for a walk on the beach, Hero?"

Once again, Hero remembered he was with Missy now, not Amanda. "Uh, I guess another time," Hero told Keera slowly, as if mesmerized by Missy's hypnotic stare.

The color rose high in Amanda's face. She was glad it was dark so no one would see. Refusing to even look at Hero and Missy, Amanda yanked open her car door, got in, and slammed it shut.

Without a word, Keera followed suit.

Who wants him to come anyway? Amanda thought furiously to herself, turning the key so hard that she almost flooded the gas tank.

Amanda's car sped down Cliff Road. For a brief second, she thought she saw the flickering shadow of a lone figure sprinting away from Missy's car at the bottom of the road.

"Did you see that, Keera?" Amanda asked quickly.

"See what?" Keera asked, lost in her own thoughts.

"That shadow leaving Missy's car," Amanda said, checking her rearview mirror to see if she could see anything else.

But, as quickly as it had been there, it was gone.

"Are you sure you didn't see it?" Amanda asked again.

"Amanda, I didn't see anything. I don't even know what you're talking about," Keera told her.

"Okay, okay. Maybe this whole Halloween thing is getting to me. Forget it, there's nothing there. On to the Torch Club!"

# Chapter Fourteen

Keera peered through the smoky haze that hung like a cloud over the room. As Amanda and Keera walked through the cavelike Torch Club looking for Jamar, the girls were greeted by the leering faces of guys standing by the bar, dragging hard on their cigarettes and clutching beer bottles.

The girls giggled nervously to each other. "Amanda, if you squint your eyes just right, don't the guys lined up on their barstools look like huge babies in high chairs, sucking their thumbs and waving baby bottles?" Keera asked.

"You're right," Amanda whispered back with a wide grin. "Where's Jamar?" she asked.

"I don't know. Backstage, I guess," Keera answered.

"Why don't we go sit down over there in the corner?" Amanda said, pointing to a small, cramped table by the wall. Keera nodded, and they threaded their way through the crowded room.

"And now, by special invitation, making their first appearance at the Torch Club, the sound you've been waiting for—The JellyJam Band," announced the tired-looking M.C.

Keera and Amanda clapped. A few hoots came from the rest of the audience, but nobody stopped talking or shouting.

As soon as the music started, the crowd seemed to get louder. It was as if they wanted to be heard over the music, instead of listening to it.

"If you're gonna sit, you gotta order," a waitress shouted to Keera over the music and the noise.

"I'll take a diet Coke," Keera said quietly, not wanting to interrupt the band's playing.

"Make that two," Amanda added.

"That it?" the waitress asked, disgusted.

Keera nodded her head and craned her neck, trying to watch Jamar.

"This place isn't exactly what I expected," Amanda shouted into Keera's ear.

"I know. Nick Ganos told Jamar this was where he got his big break. Maybe this was a classier place in those days. This crowd doesn't even seem to be listening."

Jamar's eyes lit up as soon as he spotted Keera. He couldn't deny it—he was glad Keera was there. Jamar smiled at her, knowing that she and Amanda were practically the only people in the room listening to the JellyJam sound. But the smile died on Jamar's lips when he saw who was heading toward Keera's table.

I can't believe she would do this to me, Jamar said, almost losing the thread of the music and earning himself a nasty stare from Rogue.

"Keera! What are you doing here?" Jordan Harris asked, coming up behind her.

"Jordan!" Keera said, all flustered. "What are you doing here?"

"Oh, I come here a lot, usually with the guys," Jordan said with a wave of his hand. Beer sloshed out of the bottle he was holding.

Then he looked expectantly over at Amanda.

"Oh, this is Amanda Townsend. Amanda, Jordan Harris," Keera said.

"Hey, Jordan Harris, of course," Amanda said with a big smile.

"Hey, Amanda," Jordan said. "I've seen you around school a lot. Your friend, Samantha, is on the cheerleading squad with Maya."

"Maya?" Keera asked.

"Yeah, you know, my girlfriend, Maya Turner. Here she comes now." Jordan pointed to a tall, willowy beauty who was heading their way.

Jordan introduced Maya around. Maya's unblinking, almond-shaped eyes calmly sized up Keera and Amanda before she purred, "Hello."

"Well, it's been nice to see you, Keera, although I never would have expected to find you here," Jordan said as he got up. "I thought you'd be home studying. Catch you next week—we'll do chem."

Jordan gave Keera a quick tap under the chin, then went back to a table filled with surly-looking guys whom Keera and Amanda had never seen at school. He and Maya leaned over and whispered to the crowd, who looked back over at Keera and burst into laughter.

Keera had never been so angry and embarrassed in her life.

"You know, I don't think Jordan Harris is cute at all," Amanda said slowly. "In fact, I think Jamar is much cuter. Smarter, too."

"I think so, too," Keera said. She turned her eyes back on Jamar.

"Good thing you didn't get involved with Jordan. He's way too big a jerk," Amanda said firmly, sending Jordan a disdainful glare.

"You're right," Keera answered, never taking her eyes off Jamar.

Jamar, who had been closely watching the scene at Keera's table, realized that Jordan Harris was with someone else. A girl. He wasn't with Keera at all.

Jamar let out a deep breath. Maybe he'd been wrong all along about Keera and Jordan. Maybe . . .

For the rest of the night, Jamar and the band played their hearts out. But their efforts were lost on the crowd. Nevertheless, the girls stayed till the bitter end. By one o'clock the room had cleared out except for JellyJam, the waitresses, the bartender, Keera, and Amanda.

"My mother is going to kill me for staying out so late," Keera whispered to Amanda.

"Mine's not going to be crazy about it either, if she happens to still be up," Amanda whispered back.

"Oh, my mother will be up. But we really did have to stay."

None of the band felt much like partying, since this had been the worst gig they'd ever played. Listlessly they began to disassemble their equipment as Keera and Amanda waited.

"Some great gig, huh?" Jamar said, not able to look either girl in the face.

"*I* thought it was great," Keera said. "The jerks who were here tonight don't know how to appreciate a good thing when they hear it."

"Thanks," Jamar said, ducking his head, suddenly shy.

Amanda stretched her arms out over her head. "I'm thinking it's time to head home, though. Keera, want a ride?"

Keera looked up at Jamar.

"Wait with me a minute. I've got something I want you to hear," Jamar said softly.

"Okay, I'll stay a while. But thanks, Amanda. For everything," Keera whispered, giving Amanda a quick hug.

"See you tomorrow," Amanda called as she headed out into the parking lot.

"Take a hike, guys," Jamar said to his JellyJam buddies. "Keera and I have some things to discuss."

"Come on, man—you came in my Jeep, and I wanna go home," Rogue whined.

"Aw, cool it, Rogue," the drummer, Joey Q, said, coming to Jamar's defense. "I'll give you a ride home. You can get your Jeep later." He practically shoved Rogue and the other guys out of the room.

"Closing time in ten minutes," the bartender called.

"Come here," Jamar said, pulling Keera up on the stage. "This way." He led her by the hand to a battered baby grand piano hidden in the back wings of the stage.

Keera was astonished. "What is this doing here?" she asked, running her hand over the scarred wood.

"I don't know. It must be left from the days when this was a classier place," Jamar told her. He hit a few notes. "It's still playable, though, and I want to play something for you. Stand right here." Jamar poistioned her in the curve of the piano where she could see all the keys, all the strings, the entire soul of the piano laid bare before her.

Keera stood by the heart of the piano, as Jamar played a new song. He'd written it for her yesterday, after Keera had walked out of the music room. It was a sad song about loving someone, and losing her, and never knowing why.

As the notes thrummed against the body of the piano, Keera could feel them coursing through her own body, sending an intimate vibration all the way to her heart.

Watching Jamar stroke the keys of the piano gave Keera the chills. It was as if his fingers were playing her, too. She was lost in some deep, dark place where only she and Jamar and the music mattered. The thread of the music wound around them both, drawing them closer as she stood, spellbound, while he played.

The notes faded away. Keera blinked as if waking from a dream.

"Closing time," the bartender interrupted rudely, jingling his keys.

"We're outta here," Jamar said quietly. Side by side, he and Keera walked out of the Torch Club and headed for Rogue's Jeep.

As they stood at the car door, alone in the parking lot under the moonlit sky, Jamar took Keera in his arms and held her close. Her arms went up around his neck. Ever so slowly, Jamar brought his lips to Keera's mouth and kissed her.

Keera's lips returned his kiss, slowly at first, then with greater passion as they clung to each other in the cool night air. Their breath came faster and faster as their kisses grew hungrier. Finally, they pulled apart.

Jamar held Keera's face in his hands, looking deeply into her sea-green eyes, searching for something.

"What is it?" Keera asked breathlessly.

"I just want to make sure you know it's me that you're kissing," Jamar answered.

Keera looked at Jamar in surprise. All of a sudden Keera realized he knew about Jordan. But how?

Keera's face flushed. Returning Jamar's gaze, she replied with quiet certainty, "I love *you*, Jamar. I really do love you."

Closing his eyes, Jamar pulled her to him, folding her body against his.

"And I love you," Jamar whispered into her hair. "More than you'll ever know."

After several minutes, they climbed into the Jeep. They rode in silence. For the first time since she'd known him, Jamar didn't turn on the radio and fiddle with the stations.

Something had happened between them tonight, something like magic. And neither one of them wanted to say or do anything that might break the spell.

"Well, I guess I should go in," Keera said reluctantly, when Jamar pulled up in front of her house. The light in her parents' bedroom was still shining—a bad sign for Keera.

Jamar stayed her movement, placing his hand on her arm.

"Keera . . ." he started to say.

"Yes?"

"I—I just want you to know . . ." Jamar began again.

Keera waited expectantly. She wasn't sure what Jamar was going to say, but she hoped it wouldn't be about Jordan Harris.

"Thank you for being there tonight," Jamar finally said. "It could have been the worst night of my life. But instead, because of you, it was probably the best."

Tenderly Keera put her cool hand against Jamar's warm cheek. "You're welcome. I wouldn't have missed it for the world."

Jamar brought Keera's palm to his lips.

"Good night, Keera," Jamar said simply.

"Good night, Jamar."

Keera got out of the car and stepped lightly up the porch to her house. Turning, she waved one last good-bye, then slipped inside, steeling herself to face a different sort of music.

# Chapter Fifteen

*E*arlier that evening, at the Bluff, Missy practically had to drag Hero down to the beach for a walk.

"Oh, Hero, isn't it beautiful out tonight? The moon is so big and yellow," Missy said, chattering about anything to keep Hero's attention off the Bluff and on her.

But Hero was barely listening to Missy as they walked along the beach. Instead, he was remembering the first night he and Amanda had gotten together, right here, below Cliffside Bluff. Just when he'd thought he had absolutely no chance with her whatsoever, Amanda had appeared to him as if in a dream, rising up out of the sea foam with her hair whipping in the wind.

Hero would never forget the salty, sweet taste of Amanda's lips when he'd kissed her that first time. They were salty with the taste of the sea and her tears, after Tyler had run him off the cliff during their motorcycle race.

Hero looked up to the Bluff, remembering the sheer drop down the road along the other side. Squinting against the floodlights that rimmed the cliff's edge, Hero thought he saw a quick, blurred shadow moving along the Bluff.

"Hey, I'm over this way," Missy said. She took Hero's chin in her hands, pulling his face close to hers and surprising him by covering his mouth passionately with her own.

"What's this all about?" Hero asked, lightly encircling Missy with his arms.

"What do you want it to be about?" Missy asked, putting her arms around Hero's neck, while glancing anxiously up at the Bluff.

"I don't know," Hero said. He removed Missy's arms from his neck and stepped back to look out to sea.

Suddenly, he felt a chill creep along his neck, almost as if someone's icy fingers were stroking him. Involuntarily, he shuddered.

Missy glanced over at the Bluff. Tyler was outlined against the night sky, kneeling at the edge of the cliff and signaling to let her know he was done placing rocks and other obstacles along the edge of the cliff, and rewiring the lights.

Missy turned to Hero and said, "I'm cold. I guess this wasn't such a great idea after all. Let's go back to my car and get warm."

Hero walked Missy to her car, which she had parked at the bottom of Cliff Road. "Want a ride up the hill?" Missy asked.

"No, thanks. I can make it—and I better go turn off those floodlights before the bulbs burn out and we're out of luck for tomorrow's show," Hero said. He gave Missy a quick good-bye kiss and hurried up the road to the Bluff.

After shutting off the floodlights, Hero looked around the Bluff. In the darkness, it looked a lot more sinister than it had while they were performing the re-enactment.

Suddenly Hero heard a whirring

sound. He'd left the camera running the whole time!

I was sure I'd shut this thing off after the show, Hero said to himself, annoyed at his own carelessness. Quickly, Hero shut off the camera and popped the tape into his pocket. He would take it to the station tomorrow so everyone could review the performance.

As he turned to go, Hero again felt a menacing presence, almost right behind him. Then a whiff of cold air passed through him. Looking around quickly, Hero thought he saw a shadow move in the bushes.

You're really hallucinating now, he scolded himself. You're acting almost as crazy as Amanda does about this stuff. Hero turned up the collar on his leather jacket, pulled on his helmet, and jumped onto his bike.

But no matter how he tried, Hero couldn't shake the feeling that something bad was lurking at the Bluff.

Tearing off the black ski mask he'd been wearing, Tyler hungrily sought

Missy's mouth as they clung to each other in the small dark space of Missy's car.

"Is it all taken care of?" Missy whispered, running her hands through Tyler's tousled hair.

"Everything's ready," Tyler murmured. He wriggled out of the close-fitting black turtleneck he'd put on to keep from being seen as he performed his stealthy job of sabotaging the set.

"Are you sure?" Missy asked.

"I'm sure. Nothing can go wrong," Tyler said. Then he covered Missy's mouth with his own. Tonight there would be no more talking about their plans for tomorrow.

# Chapter Sixteen

*T*he next morning was Halloween. Amanda slept in since she'd been out so late the night before. Sometime around noon, a huge weight dropped right into the middle of Amanda's bed, practically crushing her.

Amanda's eyes flew open. Only inches from her face was a hideous ghoul, with pale, peeling skin, dark, hollow eyes, and stringy, yellow hair.

"Prepare to die . . . . ." warned a muffled voice from behind the mask.

"Get a life, Kit," Amanda said, rolling over and intending to go back to sleep.

"Gee, you're a whole lot of fun," Amanda's younger sister complained good-naturedly. "Don't you think this is scary? It's what I'm wearing to the Club party tonight. I figure this outfit will keep things lively."

"Hmmmm," Amanda said, snuggling back down into the covers. I wonder what kind of costume Hero's going to wear to the dance? Amanda thought. Then she remembered with a jolt that she wasn't going to the dance with Hero. She was going with Tyler.

"Hey, sleepyhead. What are you going to be for Halloween?" Kit asked, throwing a pillow at Amanda's head.

"Cut it out. I told you, I'm dressing up like Mariah Wiley," Amanda said, burying herself under the covers.

"Oh, that's right, for your spooky Halloween show. So, when are you getting up? It's almost twelve-thirty already."

"What?" Amanda exploded, flinging back the satin, cream-colored sheets and coverlet. "Why didn't anybody wake me?" she wailed. She grabbed a faded pair of jeans with holes in the knees and pulled on an oversized Cliffside High sweatshirt.

"I've got to be at the gym by one to make sure the booths are set up and the final decorations are done, and then I've got to get over to KSS for a final prep session before the show," Amanda chattered on, brushing out her ash-blond-hair and then scooping it up into a high ponytail.

"Dad wanted to wake you before he left for golf, but Mother told him that if you were old enough to stay out until two in the morning, you were too old to need a wake-up call from your parents," Kit explained.

"Thanks a lot, Mom," Amanda said sarcastically to the air. She quickly washed her face and brushed her teeth, pulled on her sneakers, and headed for the door.

Ten minutes later, Amanda drove into the parking lot of Cliffside High and raced breathlessly to the gym. To her total and complete relief, she saw that everything had proceeded according to plan, even though she wasn't around to supervise. The haunted house booth was almost fully "haunted," the apple-bobbing barrels were being rolled into position, the fortunetelling booth was in the works, and all the volunteers were busy working.

"Hey, Amanda."

Amanda turned quickly at the sound of her name. "Hero!" she said with surprise.

"How's it going?" Hero asked, surveying the busy scene.

"Pretty good. Great, actually," Amanda answered. "It's almost as if the whole thing has taken on a life of its own and doesn't even need me."

"Does this mean you actually have some free time?" Hero asked with a slight smile.

"I guess so," Amanda said.

Then she realized that this was Saturday and Hero didn't have to be at school at all. "Hey, what are you hanging around for? Waiting for Missy?" Amanda asked, pretending indifference.

Hero scowled. "No, I'm not waiting for Missy. Missy doesn't keep me waiting."

Amanda's eyes flashed.

"Oh, hey, listen. Forget I said that," Hero said. "Look, Amanda, I came by to see if you could use any help."

"You did?" Amanda asked, totally surprised.

"Yeah. But it looks like you've got it all covered, so I guess I'll be heading out," Hero said, turning to go.

"Hero, wait. You came by looking for me?" Amanda asked hesitantly.

"I've always said you were a quick study," Hero said with a grin.

"Thanks a lot, you," Amanda said, slapping Hero playfully on the arm.

Hero grabbed Amanda's hand and held it mid-slap. Their eyes locked. All at once, Amanda was conscious of the way Hero's warm, hard hands felt against her cool, smooth skin.

Suddenly, Amanda wished that Hero would take her in his arms the way he used to and cover her face, her neck, her lips with his hungry, searching kisses. Amanda ached to feel his strong arms tight around her waist. She wanted to reach over and tenderly push back that lock of hair that was always falling in his eyes.

"Hero . . . I . . ." Amanda began.

But before she could finish her thought, she heard someone call, "Amanda! Hero! Hi!" Running toward them was Samantha Walker.

"Oh, have you made up with her, too? Are you back to being best friends again—first with Tyler, now with Samantha?" Hero asked coldly.

"What if I have?" Amanda asked, annoyed with Hero for being so obnoxious.

Hero shrugged. "Nothing. It's your life. And I just remembered, I'm not in it." Hero walked away. "See you at the KSS meeting."

Amanda bit her lip as tears of anger and frustration welled in her eyes. Hero wasn't being fair. She hadn't asked Samantha to come over to them.

"Hey, Amanda. Hope I wasn't interrupting anything with you and Hero," Samantha said.

"Even if you were, it doesn't matter now," Amanda said bitterly. "So, what's up?" Amanda asked in a cool voice.

"Look, Amanda. I know we haven't talked much this year, but I really do miss you," Samantha said. "Can't we just go back to the way things used to be? I promise, I'll never do anything to hurt you again."

Amanda looked hard at Samantha. *Why am I still so mad at her?* Amanda asked herself. *After all, I have forgiven Tyler, and I do miss talking to Samantha.*

"Oh, why not?" Amanda surrendered.

"Great. I've got so much to tell you." Samantha started to chatter away. "You'll never guess who I saw together a few days ago."

"Who?"

"Tyler and Missy!" Samantha crowed.

Amanda's eyes burned angrily into Samantha's.

"Samantha Walker, you are a gossip and a liar. You know I'm seeing Tyler now, but you just can't get past the fact that he doesn't even know you're alive. First you say you want to be my friend. Then you start doing the same thing all over again, trying to make me jealous. And I can't believe you'd make up something about Tyler and Missy, of all people. Missy is going out with Hero!" Amanda's voice rose shrilly. "Get a life, Samantha. I don't want to talk to you anymore."

Amanda turned away in fury and headed straight for her car.

"Amanda, wait. Listen to me," Samantha called after her.

Amanda kept on walking.

"You'll see, I'm right about them," Samantha called after her.

Without looking back, Amanda yanked open her car door, got in, and slammed it shut. She sat for a moment trembling with . . . she didn't know what. Could what Samantha said actually be true?

Pushing the thought from her head, Amanda started her car and zoomed out of the parking lot.

Amanda was so angry, she didn't notice Missy driving in the opposite direction with Tyler close beside her.

Tyler had a satisfied smile on his face as he sat with his arm draped over Missy's shoulders. Anyone who wasn't blind could see that the two of them looked bleary, sandy, and disheveled—almost as if they'd spent the entire night sleeping on the beach.

Samantha, watching Amanda drive away, definitely wasn't blind.

Oh, if only I had my camera, I'd take a picture of this pair and prove to Amanda that there's something going on, Samantha thought. She was dying to know what Missy and Tyler were up to. And Samantha intended to find out.

# *Chapter Seventeen*

*L*ater that day, all the KSS staffers gathered around the control room monitors, ready to screen yesterday's rehearsal of the Halloween special.

Hero and Amanda pointedly sat on opposite sides of the room. Keera and Jamar, on the other hand, looked like they'd been glued together at the hip. Amanda couldn't help feeling envious when she saw how dreamy-eyed and in love Jamar and Keera seemed to be.

Sighing, Amanda threw a brief glance at Hero. His gaze met hers for a moment. Amanda ventured a small smile, but Hero shifted his gaze and focused on the monitors instead.

Hardening her expression, Amanda turned to stare at the screen as well. Forget Hero. Think Tyler, Amanda reminded herself.

"I've got to hand it to you folks," Drew said when the performance was over. "That was a great job. I really like the combined use of those two camera angles, Hero," Drew added.

"Thanks," Hero said.

"Well, that about wraps it up. I'll see you guys tonight at the Bluff for the real thing, after your dance," Drew said, getting up from his seat.

"Hey, would you look at that?" Hero said with a low whistle, pointing to the monitor.

At first the picture seemed to be whirling around, as though the camera had dropped off the tripod and someone was trying to set it back up. But there was no one onscreen. All they could hear were some off-camera grunts and groans.

"What's going on?" Keera asked, looking frightened.

"It's the legend," Amanda whispered in awe.

"Don't be ridiculous," Hero said. But he, like the others, was glued to his seat, watching and listening.

As the tape kept rolling, a black-clad

figure roamed back and forth in the distance, like a shadow flickering across the lens. It seemed to be moving with no particular purpose, kneeling here and there along the Bluff's edge, darting noiselessly up and down the cliff. At one point it stood at the very top of the point, waving its arms above its head.

Then, as mysteriously as it had appeared, the shadow disappeared over the edge of the cliff.

Then there was nothing but stillness, and everything went black. A few moments later, they all heard Hero's voice say "Damn" under his breath as he discovered the camera was still running. Then a click, and the tape was done.

Amanda's eyes were as round as saucers. Keera was pressed against Jamar's chest, trembling and looking pale. Jamar was trying to appear unafraid, but even he was a shade paler than usual. Only Hero didn't look frightened. His eyes were narrowed to slits as he stared skeptically at the monitor.

"Want to run that by us again?" Drew asked hoarsely.

"Sure," Hero said, punching the rewind and play buttons.

One more time, they watched the performance after the performance.

"That's definitely a spirit of some sort," Amanda said. "I bet it's Clarissa's spirit."

"Don't be maudlin, Amanda. There must be some other explanation," Keera insisted. "Isn't there?" She looked around for assurance from everyone else.

Drew shrugged his shoulders. Jamar looked helpless.

Hero, who had been paying very close attention to the screen, said, "That's definitely a person."

"How can you say that?" Amanda asked. "Haven't you been listening? It's the spirit, the one that's been shoving people off the Bluff for almost a century. And it's waiting there for us, because we're going to let everyone know the truth about what really happened."

"It's a person!" Hero insisted. "I

knew I felt something last night when I was up there by myself, but I couldn't put my finger on it."

"You just won't admit that there are some things in this world that can't be explained," Amanda said.

"Don't be ridiculous, Amanda," Hero said scornfully. "Of course, there are no such things as spirits—only people who believe in them."

"Well, then how do you explain what we just saw?" Keera asked.

"I'm not sure, yet," Hero said, frowning to himself. "I can't imagine why anyone would be up there messing around on the Bluff, but I'm working on it," Hero said, more to himself than to the others. "I'm working on it."

The others filed out of the control room, eager to put some distance between themselves and the tape.

"That was creepy," Keera said, grabbing Amanda's arm with her cold hands as they walked into the main office.

"Oooh, don't make me jump," Amanda said, reacting to Keera's icy hands.

"What do you think, Drew?" Jamar wanted to know.

Drew shrugged. "I couldn't tell you. I've never seen anything like this. I don't believe in spirits or anything like that, but who really knows? One thing is for sure, though."

"What's that?" Keera asked.

"We'll find out tonight." Drew grinned.

"Great. And maybe we'll all end up dead," Amanda muttered.

"Stop that nonsense, girl," Keera scolded her. "Nobody's going to end up dead. It's just a legend, a story, old news from another century. Besides, there'll be hundreds of people around, watching. Nothing's going to happen."

"We'll see," Amanda said thoughtfully.

"Hey, Hero, are you coming?" Jamar called into the control room as he and Keera headed for the exit.

"You all go ahead," Hero said, waving them away. "I'm going to watch this a few more times before I'm outta here."

"Remember to lock up, then," Drew

called as he followed Jamar and Keera out the door.

"Hero . . ." Amanda began.

"Later, Amanda," Hero said, unable to tear his eyes away from the screen. He was standing so close to the monitors, he was practically inside them.

"Later, Hero," Amanda said, turning to go. But she couldn't escape the feeling of dread that had begun in the pit of her stomach and was spreading quickly to her heart.

Amanda returned home to an empty house. Mrs. Townsend and Kit were at the Club, and Mr. Townsend was still out playing golf.

Slowly, Amanda climbed the long marble staircase to the second floor and headed toward her room. The house seemed ominously quiet in the fading afternoon light. Shadows fell across the hall floor.

Quickly, Amanda slipped into her room and pulled off her clothes. Even more quickly, she stepped into the shower and began shampooing her hair, scrubbing hard, hoping to erase the shadowy image of the spirit on the Bluff.

By the time Amanda finished showering, the house was completely dark. Expertly wrapping her long, wet hair in a towel, she sat at her pink marble vanity table and studied the tintype her mother had given her of Mariah Wiley. Then she began to put on the makeup for her costume that night.

An hour later, Amanda was just about to put the last pin in her upswept hair when the phone by her bed rang.

Keeping her head straight so she wouldn't ruin her hair, Amanda went to answer the phone. As she picked it up, she heard a click.

"Hello," Amanda said into the phone. There was silence.

"Hello," Amanda said, more insistently. Again, there was no answer.

Amanda could almost feel the other person breathing on the other end of the phone. But despite several more "hello's" there was no response.

"Come on, Jamar. Keera? This isn't funny. I know I said I believed in spirits, but this isn't a cool joke. Kit? Is that you?" Amanda asked, half-expecting to hear her sister's laughter on the other end.

But all Amanda heard was another loud click. Then the phone went dead.

"Hello?" Amanda whispered into the telephone, genuinely scared now. But her only answer was the insistent drone of the dial tone.

Amanda lay down the phone with a trembling hand. The call must have been some random Halloween prank, which just caught her at a bad time, she decided.

From her closet, Amanda took out the bridal dress that looked just like the one Mariah Wiley had been wearing that Halloween night in 1894.

It wasn't the same dress, of course. This was her youngest sister's wedding dress. It had been tucked away in an old trunk in the attic, lovingly preserved in special paper. Mrs. Townsend had had it cleaned so Amanda could wear it to the costume ball.

Amanda slipped the heavy cream-colored lace and brocade dress over her head, careful not to destroy her hair.

The dress fit Amanda perfectly. As she gazed at her reflection in the full-length mirror inside her closet door, she almost didn't recognize herself. With her upswept hair, the makeup, and the dress, Amanda looked more like Mariah Wiley than the tintype itself.

At that moment, the phone rang again. Amanda snatched the receiver. "Hello?" she practically yelled into the phone.

"Amanda?"

Relief flooded through Amanda's body. "Tyler. I'm so glad it's you."

"I couldn't remember if I was driving you to the dance, or if you're driving on your own," Tyler asked.

Amanda thought about it for a minute. She didn't remember discussing the issue with Tyler at all.

It would be better if she took her own car, Amanda considered. Then she wouldn't have to rely on Tyler to get to the Bluff. But her nerves were so shaky that Amanda decided she'd rather have Tyler's company than none at all.

"Oh, Tyler, you're a lifesaver. I'd love to ride over with you. I'll be ready in fifteen minutes," Amanda said gratefully.

"I'll be there," Tyler said smoothly. He smiled at Missy as he replaced the phone in its cradle.

"You're a genius, Tyler," Missy said, giving Tyler a long, hard kiss. Then, looking at her watch, she said, "I better run. What do you think of how I look?"

Tyler surveyed Missy in her tight-fitting peach-colored Homecoming Queen gown, which showed every curve of Missy's well-formed body. Her shiny auburn hair and her cat-green eyes glowed with the excitement of her imminent and satisfying revenge on Amanda Townsend, whom she had despised for as long as she could remember.

"Come here," Tyler said softly. "I'll show you what I think."

"Gently, Tyler. I don't want to mess up my dress," Missy said, folding herself into Tyler's arms for one last kiss.

"That's enough," Missy said, attempting to pull herself out of Tyler's grasp. "We wouldn't want to tarnish the Homecoming Queen image," she added with a sly smile.

"No, of course not," Tyler said, insisting on one more kiss before releasing her.

"So, you'll meet up with Amanda at the Bluff and I'll get there with Hero. No talking to each other during the dance, right?" Missy asked.

"Right," Tyler agreed. "Although it's going to be hard keeping my mind on Amanda instead of you," Tyler said, moving closer.

"Later, Tyler," Missy insisted as they headed outside.

"Not too much later," Tyler said.

# Chapter Eighteen

"Hey, Tyler," Amanda said, answering the door. Tyler was dressed in a black turtleneck, black jeans, and black sneakers. "What are you supposed to be?"

"A cat burglar, what else?" Tyler said, taking Amanda's arm. "You look amazing, Amanda."

"Thank you, sir," Amanda said, giving a little curtsy.

She was starting to feel more like Mariah than Amanda.

Tyler and Amanda were one of the first couples to arrive at the dance. Amanda had planned to be early, since she wanted to make sure everything was going smoothly.

After scurrying around for fifteen minutes while Tyler waited patiently,

Amanda settled gratefully into Tyler's arms as JellyJam started to play.

Several minutes later, Amanda saw Missy walk in. Amanda craned her neck, expecting to see Hero walk in behind her. But he didn't.

"Hmmmmm," Amanda said. "Looks like Missy came alone."

"Amanda, you're so beautiful, I can't see anybody else but you. If you hadn't pointed her out, I wouldn't even have known that Missy Hanover was alive. Now stop talking and let's dance," Tyler commanded, pulling Amanda closer and laying her head on his chest.

So much for what Samantha knows, Amanda said to herself, remembering how her ex-friend had tried to convince her that Missy Hanover and Tyler were a couple.

Missy floated by on her way to the punch bowl. She tried not to smile at Tyler, but she couldn't help herself. A little smirk escaped.

Tyler, seeing her smile, twisted his face into a quick secret smile of his own.

Amanda didn't notice.

Samantha Walker, who was standing by the fortuneteller's booth, did.

Amanda imagined she was Mariah Wiley at a costume ball, floating in the arms of some adoring male—perhaps even Jess Wiley, since Mariah couldn't very well have been dancing with Winston Hanover in public.

Just then, a lone figure appeared at the door, calmly surveying the scene. He was dressed up in a gray morning coat, white shirt, plum tie, and top hat. The figure stepped smartly into the gym, walking stick raised.

"Hero?" Amanda said in disbelief.

Hero spotted Amanda dancing with Tyler, and his heart sank. He'd been hoping that Amanda might have come alone.

Amanda was so stunned by how handsome Hero looked in his costume, she forgot to keep dancing. She couldn't believe how much he looked like the tintype of Winston Hanover she had lent him.

"Hey, Amanda. What are you doing?" Tyler asked, annoyed that his rhythm had been interrupted. He had just managed to convince himself it was Missy he was dancing with after all.

"I'll be back in a minute," Amanda told him.

As if drawn by some irresistible force, Amanda floated over to where Hero stood near the entrance. The noisy, crowded gymnasium melted away, and it seemed as if they were the only two people left in the world.

Hero watched Amanda approach. He, too, felt an irresistible pull toward her, greater than the one between them when they were simply Hero and Amanda.

"Amanda, you look beautiful," Hero said softly.

"So do you," Amanda replied.

"Think I'll make a convincing Winston Hanover?"

"You've convinced me," Amanda said. She gazed adoringly into Hero's eyes.

"Amanda, I've been . . ." Hero started to say.

"Hero, I wanted to . . ." Amanda started to say at the same time.

"Hero, you make a smashing Winston Hanover," Missy said, swooping in before Hero or Amanda could complete their thoughts.

In that moment, the spell was broken.

Amanda stepped back. "Well, I guess I'll be getting back to Tyler," she said, wishing that Hero would protest.

Hero's eyes flickered. "See you at the Bluff, then," he said, turning his attention to Missy.

Amanda walked slowly back to Tyler, who welcomed her back into his arms without a word of complaint.

"I'm kind of thirsty, Tyler. Do you mind if we stop dancing?" Amanda asked.

"Not at all," Tyler said, walking Amanda over to the punch bowl. "I'll be right back."

Amanda looked around the crowded gym, hoping to catch sight of Hero again, even if he was with Missy. But with all the different costumes, face masks, and people hurrying from booth to booth and through the haunted house, it was impossible.

"Great party, Amanda," people commented as they walked by. "Good job. You look wonderful."

Amanda smiled automatically at the compliments. Somehow, planning the party didn't seem all that important anymore—now that she didn't have Hero to share it with.

Glancing down at her wrist, Amanda realized she'd forgotten to put on her watch.

"What time is it?" Amanda asked a ghoulish-faced figure standing next to her.

"What time would you like it to be?" he leered back.

"It's nine o'clock," someone else answered, coming up behind Amanda.

"Keera!" Amanda said, happy to recognize a friendly face.

"Amanda, you look magnificent," Keera said in an awed tone. "You look just like that tintype of Mariah that you showed me."

"Thank you," Amanda said, lowering her eyes modestly. "Have you seen Hero?"

"Oh, definitely. You two will look

like the perfect couple for tonight's show," Keera replied. Then, seeing the two spots of color form on Amanda's cheeks at the words "perfect couple," Keera bit her lip.

"I've got Jamar's costume for Jess Wiley in the car, but it's nothing compared to Hero's," Keera said.

"I'm sure it'll be just fine," Amanda told her.

"I wonder what Missy's planning to wear for the show tonight," Keera said. "Her homecoming dress doesn't exactly make her look like a fourteen-year-old."

"I don't think there's anything that can make Missy look like a fourteen-year-old," Amanda commented. Keera giggled.

Suddenly the lights came up, and JellyJam ended its song. Jamar's voice boomed over the sound system, quieting the crowd.

"Okay, folks. This is the moment you've been waiting for—the crowning of the Haunted Homecoming Queen," he said. "We will be crowning our queen early this year so she can do her part for KSS-TV's Halloween Special—to which all of you are invited, after the dance. Vans will be leaving for the Bluff at eleven-thirty sharp—arranged by the one, the only, Amanda Townsend." Jamar pointed to Amanda, who nodded and waved as the crowd applauded.

"And now, a drum roll please," Jamar said. "Here she comes, goblins and ghouls, Miss Haunted Homecoming Queen of 1994, Missy Hanover!" The band broke into a rap version of "Miss America" as the spotlight picked up Missy walking from the entrance to the gym to the stage. She was escorted by Hero, to the sound of much applause and approving hoots.

Elegantly, Hero brought Missy up to the podium, where she climbed the steps as best she could in her tight-fitting peach gown.

"Thank you. Thank you all for electing me Homecoming Queen," Missy began.

At that moment, Amanda appeared at the edge of the stage with a dozen blood-red roses.

"The Homecoming Committee decided that this year, we wanted to present our Homecoming Queen with several gifts to show our appreciation," Amanda said mechanically. "Please take these roses as a show of our affection and appreciation." Amanda stiffly placed the flowers into Missy's outstretched arms.

"Thank you, Mandy," Missy said, then added under her breath, "for the roses, and for Hero, too!"

Amanda had had it. Her cheeks colored, and she turned on her heel and left the stage.

Jamar turned to the crowd and said, "And now, before we do the crowning, we have a special surprise. In the true spirit of Halloween, we have a new look for our Homecoming Queen."

One of the other committee members appeared from the side of the stage with what looked like a witch's head on a serving platter.

Missy gasped in horror as the crowd in the gym laughed uproariously.

"Very funny," Missy said, realizing the "head" was actually a mask. "But I don't think it goes with what I'm wearing." She pushed the mask away.

"Oh, come on, Missy, be a sport. Put it on—it's Halloween," people shouted from the crowd.

Knowing she had no choice, Missy reluctantly put the witch's mask on. It made a stunning contrast to her gown.

Everyone laughed and stamped their feet in approval. This certainly beat the traditional crowning ceremony!

Missy was about to step down, when Jamar held her back. "Wait, oh Queen, there is but one more offering you must accept. The most important offering of all," he said. Then Jamar held out the rhinestone crown and deposited it on top of the witch's hat. The crowd in the gym went crazy.

Missy's crown slipped a bit as she leaned on Hero's arm to come down from the stage. As soon as she reached the gym floor, she whipped the witch's mask off, and shoved it into Amanda's arms.

"Thanks for arranging the Homecoming crowning," Missy said, smiling sweetly. "It was a great goof."

"We thought we'd do something a little different this year," Amanda said, smiling mischievously as she held up the witch's mask.

"It was definitely different," Missy agreed through gritted teeth.

At that moment, JellyJam's music exploded throughout the gym. "Hero, wouldn't you like to have the next dance with the Homecoming Queen?" Missy asked, placing her hand possessively on Hero's broad chest.

"Shouldn't you be wearing your crown, then?" Amanda asked sweetly, offering the crown and witch's mask back to Missy.

"No, thanks, Mandy," Missy remarked. "Consider this my way of passing the crown on to you."

And with that Missy pulled Hero onto the dance floor.

Just then, Tyler glided up behind Amanda. "There you are," Tyler said, encircling Amanda with his arms. "Let's dance."

The two couples kept their distance from each other on the dance floor. But their eyes couldn't stop seeking each other out.

Looking over at Tyler in his cat burglar outfit, Hero had a momentary flash of déjà vu. He'd seen an image somewhere that reminded him of the way Tyler looked . . .

But before he could place it, Missy pulled his head back and kissed him lightly on the lips.

"Pay attention to your queen," she admonished him.

"Yes, ma'am," Hero said, forgetting about Tyler for the moment.

Keera stood off to the side, watching the two couples dance. Even though it had been several weeks, she still couldn't get used to seeing Missy with Hero and Amanda with Tyler. It just felt wrong to her, no matter how often she'd seen them together.

"Interesting couple—Missy and Tyler," someone commented at Keera's elbow. "Dangerous, too," the voice added.

"You mean, Missy and Hero," Keera said, whirling around to see who had spoken. But all she saw was a flash of gold earrings, bright clothing, and a red scarf.

Looking back at the dance floor, Keera caught the glimmer of a smile exchanged between Tyler and Missy.

Don't be ridiculous, Keera thought to herself. Just because someone in a gypsy costume comes up and says something, you're imagining all sorts of things.

Determined to put the gypsy's words out of her mind, Keera went over to remind Jamar it was time to get ready for the show at the Bluff.

The shuttle vans stood ready outside the gym door, waiting to take everyone to the Bluff for the KSS-TV Haunted Halloween special.

Almost everyone piled out of the gym at the same time. In all of the confusion, Tyler and Missy were separated from Hero and Amanda.

"I need to speak to you," Tyler whispered to Missy.

"Meet me around the back in two minutes," Missy answered. Then she disappeared into the crowd.

* * *

Amanda helped supervise the exodus onto the vans. When the last one pulled out, Amanda looked around for Tyler. But she couldn't find him in the darkened parking lot.

Remembering that Keera and Jamar had already left, Amanda began to worry how she was going to get to the Bluff. Then she spotted Hero straddling his motorcycle, getting ready to roll.

Amanda smiled at the sight of Hero, dressed like Winston Hanover in his gentleman's coat. The only sign of the real Hero was the tips of his worn, black leather boots sticking out from under his pants.

Hero looked up to find Amanda standing before him. "Where's Tyler?" he asked.

Amanda shrugged. "Where's Missy?" she asked.

Hero shrugged. "Need a ride?"

"If you can spare one," Amanda said.

"Sure, get on."

Carefully holding up her dress, Amanda lifted her leg over the cycle seat and fitted herself against Hero's back.

Hero gunned the engine. His heart was racing almost as quickly.

Seated behind Hero, Amanda's heart was pounding so hard, she thought he'd be able to feel it against his back.

"What are we doing?" Amanda shouted over the noise of the engine.

"What?" Hero asked, pulling out of the parking spot.

"Never mind," Amanda shouted back.

As Hero and Amanda pulled out, Tyler and Missy arrived at the front of the gym. Realizing that they had missed their opportunity to go with Hero and Amanda, they quickly went to their separate cars and raced up to the Bluff.

Only one person remained. The girl with the gold earrings, red scarf, and bright-colored clothing—carrying a camera.

Quickly, she slipped into her car and raced up to the Bluff after the others.

# Chapter Nineteen

As Hero and Amanda rode up to the Bluff, they could see the crowds assembling.

"Thanks for the ride, Hero," Amanda said softly as she slid off the seat.

"No problem," Hero replied just as softly, looking directly at her.

There was an awkward silence, which was shattered as soon as Keera and Jamar spotted them.

"Hey, you two," Keera cried. "Let's get going. Everybody's waiting!"

"How do I look?" Jamar asked, showing off his outfit.

"Just like Jess Wiley," Amanda said, laughing. "If you don't watch out, Mariah might end up falling in love with you!" she teased.

"Come on, guys. Let's get into

position," Keera urged them. "Does anybody know where Missy is?"

Hero and Amanda looked at each other. Then they looked at Keera and shrugged.

"Great, just great," Keera muttered.

Somehow, by eleven-forty, everything and everyone was in position.

Missy had managed to do a quick change. Despite Amanda and Keera's doubts, she had found a demure gingham dress that did made her look younger. She had also forced her thick red hair into two high pigtails, one on each side of her head, which bounced saucily when she moved.

As Keera stepped into the spotlight, the crowd hushed. Keera began her introduction, telling about the legend, the spirits, and the contradictory stories surrounding the deaths of Mariah Wiley, Winston Hanover, Jess Wiley, and Clarissa Hanover.

"Tonight, to add to the mystery, the part of Mariah Wiley will be played by Amanda Townsend, a descendant of Mariah. And the part of Clarissa

Hanover will be played by her descendant, Melissa Hanover.

"And now, I ask you to close your eyes and go back in time with me, to Allhallows Eve, 1894," Keera said in a hushed voice.

As the play unfolded, a black-clad figure prowled stealthily just beyond the glare of the floodlights, checking on the newly added wires connected to a switch he carried in his hands.

As the play progressed and Missy crept into the bushes to watch the rest of the drama unfold, she felt a cold hand tap her on the shoulder. It was Tyler. He put his hands to his lips to signal that she not say a word.

"It's all set," Tyler mouthed. Then he leaned into the bushes to give Missy a deep, long kiss.

Suddenly, a flashbulb popped about twenty feet away from them.

Surprised, Tyler and Missy pulled apart, looking around for the source of the flash. But there was nothing but a blur of red and gold disappearing into the dark.

"I'll be back," Tyler mouthed, hand-ing Missy the auxiliary switch. "You know what to do."

Then, he moved out of the bushes to investigate the unexpected flash.

At eleven-fifty-five, Mariah and Winston were startled by the appearance of Jess Wiley interrupting their passionate embrace. But just as Mariah and Winston stepped backward toward the cliff's edge, the floodlights shorted out. Sparks flew, there was a smell of burning wire, and the whole Bluff was plunged into darkness.

Stumbling in the dark near the cliff's edge, Amanda screamed. And then there was a loud thump.

Hero shouted, grabbing at the empty space beside him.

The crowd stirred uneasily, unsure whether or not this was part of the show.

"Amanda, Hero, Jamar!" Keera shouted, suddenly realizing that something had gone wrong.

A minute later, a blood-curdling scream came from the wooded thicket near the path.

"Amanda, where are you?" Hero cried hoarsely.

But Amanda did not reply.

"Hero," Jamar called. "I'm going to try to find a way to get the lights back on. Don't move!"

Ignoring Jamar's warning, Hero crawled along the cliff's edge, feeling the rim with his fingers. There seemed to be a lot more rocks scattered there than there had been the night before. Had someone placed them there deliberately, so Amanda would fall?

"Amanda, love. I'm here, Amanda. Don't move, I'm coming. I'm coming for you, Amanda," Hero called over and over.

As he inched along in the darkness, a thought came unbidden into Hero's mind. The shadowy image that had flickered at the edge of his sight last night and on the rehearsal tape—

"Tyler!" Hero gasped. "It was Tyler."

Just then, Hero heard a small groan and the sound of pebbles shifting and sliding down the cliff.

"Amanda. Don't move. I'll be right there." He tried to guess how far he was from Amanda and if he could get to her before the unthinkable happened.

As if by magic, the floodlights suddenly came back on.

There, with one arm and leg dangling over the cliff's edge, lay Amanda Townsend, barely conscious.

Hero knelt by her side and gently scooped her up, pulling her to safety. He could see that she had a large gash on the side of her face, just below the temple, where a rock must have cut her when she fell. Blood trickled down her face and into her hair, staining the ivory lace and brocade of her dress.

Oblivious to the crowd that gathered around them, Hero pulled a white handkerchief from his pocket and tenderly held it to her head to stop the blood.

Keera and Jamar rushed over to Hero's side. "What happened?" Jamar asked.

"When the lights went out, she must have stumbled and hit her head on a rock. I found her lying on the edge. In another minute, she would have been . . ." Hero couldn't finish his sentence.

"Okay, everybody. Everything's going to be okay," Jamar said to the crowd pushing in to get a look at Amanda. "Show's over. The vans will be pulling out shortly, so thanks for coming—and Happy Halloween."

"Can she hear us?" Keera asked Hero, peering into Amanda's pale face.

"I don't know," Hero said, fighting back tears. He bent closer to Amanda.

"Amanda. It's Hero. I hope you can hear me, Amanda," Hero said, his voice a whisper. Then he put his lips to her ear. "I love you. I love you. I love only you," he repeated, over and over, into Amanda's ear.

Suddenly, Amanda's eyes flew open. She winced and turned her head slightly to gaze into Hero's eyes.

"Hero," she murmured.

"I'm here, Amanda," Hero said, holding her face in his hands.

"Oh, Hero," Amanda said as she struggled to sit up. "Who turned out the lights?"

Hero smiled and held her close.

"Guess we forgot to pay the bill," he answered.

Amanda gave a short, painful laugh.

"Sssh, don't laugh," Hero told her.

"Don't say anything funny then," Amanda admonished him.

Then she looked up into his dark brown eyes and finally felt like she'd come home.

"Hero, I'm so sorry," Amanda said. "Sorry about Tyler . . ."

"It doesn't matter now," Hero started to say. Then he remembered the connection he had made.

Tyler!

Just then, from the wooded thicket, four people emerged: a burly-looking guy from the hockey team at school, hauling a black-clad figure; and a gypsy, wearing a red scarf, gold earrings, a bright skirt, and a smashed camera around her neck, dragging a girl with two high pigtails.

"What's going on?" Keera asked.

"We found these two in the woods, holding this!" the gypsy said, brandishing the auxiliary switch that Tyler and Missy had used to cut off the floodlights.

"I knew it," Hero said, glaring at Tyler.

Amanda squinted hard at the gypsy. "Samantha?" Amanda asked, incredulous. "What are you doing here?"

"You wouldn't believe me when I told you about seeing Tyler and Missy together, so I wanted to prove it—with this," Samantha said, holding up the smashed camera.

"What do you mean, Tyler and Missy together?" Hero asked, narrowing his eyes.

"I've got it all here: Tyler and Missy kissing behind the gym, Tyler and Missy kissing in the bushes here, right during the middle of the show . . . or at least I *did* have it all here, before Tyler tried to wrench the camera from around my neck and ended up smashing it against a tree," Samantha said, rubbing the sore spot on her neck where Tyler had pulled the camera strap.

"Tyler, how could you do this?" Amanda asked, her violet eyes filling with tears at his betrayal.

"Oh, spare me the tears, Amanda.

You didn't get half of what you deserved. You never cared anything about me. You only care about Hero," Tyler said, practically spitting the name in her face.

Hero looked hard at Missy. "So all of this was about you and Tyler trying to get to Amanda?" he asked. Disgusted, Hero turned to Amanda and said, "Come on. Let's get you home." Then he scooped Amanda up in his arms and carried her to his motorcycle.

"So, I guess I missed everything when I fell—the screams, the sobs, the near-death incident," Amanda said with a small smile, as Hero gently placed her on his motorcycle seat.

"Are you kidding? You didn't miss a thing, Amanda. You were the main event."

"I hope now you'll believe me when I tell you about things like legends and spirits."

"Amanda," Hero said, looking deeply into her beautiful violet eyes.

"Yes," Amanda said, gazing back.

"Shut up, will you?" Hero said, leaning over to kiss her.

Amanda grabbed his hair and held him back. "Wait a minute, I have something to say to you," she said.

"Oh, yeah. What is it?" Hero asked.

Looking Hero solemnly in the face, Amanda said in a serious voice, "I've always loved you with all of my heart, and I always will—from the first moment I saw you until the day I die." Amanda recited the words of the play from memory, meaning each and every one of them.

Hero looked deeply into Amanda's eyes.

"And I vow to love you for all eternity and beyond," Hero whispered in reply.

Slowly, their lips came together, and they clung to each other in the cool autumn night—as Mariah and Winston had never been able to do.